HERETIC

Chapter One

"This is a really bad idea," Lily Fontenot whispered urgently as she crept through the trees surrounding the massive field now serving as a shuttle lot. It was late afternoon and darkness fell fast in these strange mountains. Everything on this distant planet looked similar to Earth. But the operative word was similar. The shape and size of the trees were Earthlike, yet the leaves and grasses were more blue than green. The sky, on the other hand, was a vivid teal. And large bodies of water, at least the ones Lily had seen so far, were a strange emerald green.

Thea Cline glanced back at Lily with an unrepentant smile. "Do you have somewhere else to be?"

It was a valid question. Boredom had been a serious challenge in the four weeks since leaving Earth. Since *leaving* Earth? The phrase tightened the knot of tension already twisting Lily's gut. That made it sound as if they'd had a choice. The truth was much more infuriating. Lily, along with over three thousand other human females, had been kidnapped by a band of alien mercenaries called Outcasts.

Most of the Outcasts were Rodyte or Rodyte/Bilarrian hybrids. Both species were nearly indistinguishable from humans. They were bigger than most human males and the incandescent rings in their eyes were odd, but their body shape and the arrangement of their features were so familiar that it was possible to forget they were aliens.

The purpose for the mass kidnapping was simple, and as primal as a predator's need to hunt. The Outcasts had come to this primitive planet in a barely explored sector of space to establish a settlement free from government corruption and pointless social conflicts. They wanted to live by their own rules and create a secure environment for themselves and eventually their sons and daughters. But progeny required the one thing an uninhabited planet couldn't provide—genetically compatible females.

That was where the captives came in. Each female the Outcasts kidnapped was genetically compatible with one or more of the Outcasts. To Lily's knowledge, she was the only exception. The Outcasts wanted her because she was a well-respected geneticist, and cross-species reproduction was tricky to say the least.

"What about that one?" Thea motioned toward a small shuttle near the perimeter of the field. "The hatch is open. We can walk right in."

"There could be people on that shuttle for all we know. There's probably a reason they didn't secure the ship." Lily sank deeper into the shadow of the trees, while Thea crept closer to the clearing. Thea was bold to the point of recklessness, while Lily had a tendency to overthink everything. The contrast in their personalities was one of the reasons they enjoyed each other's company. Lily was the voice of reason for hotheaded Thea, while Thea frequently urged Lily beyond the boring sameness of her comfort zone. This spontaneous quest for weapons certainly qualified. Lily had no idea what Thea intended to do with a blaster even if they managed to find one. All of Lily's logical objections hadn't deterred Thea in the least, so Lily reluctantly gave in and joined the hunt.

"There's only one way to find out." Thea tossed the challenge over her shoulder as she stepped out into the hazy sunlight.

Lily hurried after her friend, frantically looking around as she went. The first week after their arrival, they'd been confined to the ships on which they'd arrived. They'd been allowed to visit lounges, dining rooms and gymnasiums during the second and third weeks. They'd also been taken outside in shifts to a well-guarded area the captives named "the yard". By the fourth week, numerous failed escape attempts and endless hours of redundant conversations helped the captives realize they had nowhere to run. Now well-behaved females were allowed outside without an escort as long as their explorations didn't take them too far from the multi-ship complex and they checked in with security as they departed and returned. Thea seldom qualified as well-behaved, but Lily talked the guard into giving them a chance. She hoped he wouldn't be punished for his decision to let them go.

Twenty-three shuttles were scattered across the clearing with no rhyme nor reason. Lily pictured them in straight, evenly spaced rows, perhaps arranged by size or the duration of their stay on the surface. Her basic nature required order and strict control, which was one of the reasons her captivity had been so challenging. This was a good example of the overarching philosophy guiding the Outcasts. Overlord Kage Razel told his followers where to land, but left the specifics up to each individual. The fewer rules required of the Outcasts, the better they liked it. And the longer the overlord would remain in power.

Thea reached their target without incident and hurried up the steps leading to the shuttle's interior. "It's clear," she called a moment later and Lily quickly joined her inside.

Pausing to look around, Lily was surprised by her lack of reaction to the advanced technology. Three months ago this would have filled her with wonder and curiosity. Now she'd seen it all before. A Rodyte general named Garin Nox flew out from behind the moon and proved to Earth that aliens were real. Lily had been working aboard an enormous Rodyte ship when the Outcasts kidnapped her, so this two-man shuttle was far from impressive.

The pilot hadn't just left the hatch open. He'd left the ship in standby mode. The holo-matrix, a three-dimensional grid used to control everything from simple beverage kiosks to the most sophisticated ship in the Rodyte fleet, hovered in front of the pilot's seat, waiting for the next gestural command.

"Let's try to fly it." Thea's utter lack of expression made it impossible to determine if she were serious or not. "How hard could it be?"

"Harder than you could imagine." Lily dismissed the silliness with an impatient wave of her hand. "He left the ship active. He clearly doesn't expect to be here long."

Thea made a face. "Spoil sport." But she opened the nearest compartment and began her search.

Lily did the same while her analytical mind considered Thea's suggestion. "Even if we could fly the ship, where would we go? We're not even sure where we are." Escape was pointless, and dangerous. If they escaped into the surrounding wilderness, they would likely starve to death. If they didn't die of exposure first. They had nowhere to run and no one to help them. None of the Outcasts had any interest in returning to Earth. The women were stuck on a primitive planet with a bunch of mercenaries determined to "bond" with them.

Just the thought of mating with a Rodyte sent a shiver down Lily's spine. Even though they possessed incredibly advanced technology, the Outcasts were savage and aggressive, used to taking whatever they wanted without regret or mercy. She might not be able to produce offspring with any of the Outcasts, but she was still a young, healthy female. Something could happen to one of the genetically compatible females, or one of the males might not be accepted by his potential mate. Genetic compatibility didn't ensure that a couple's personalities would mesh, and some women were compatible with multiple males while some males only had one compatible female. No matter who the female chose, she was damning the other males to life without a soul-bonded mate. Such disparities had caused all sorts of complications back on Earth. It was just a matter of time before such a male shifted his focus to Lily.

She spent a lot of time thinking about the possibilities that might lead to one of the males claiming her. It was almost as if she didn't want to be left out of the coming chaos. But that was ridiculous. She was an independent female, entirely responsible for her own happiness. The idea of finding a permanent mate hadn't even entered her thinking. A twinge of guilt accompanied the assertion. She didn't like to lie to herself, but the truth was still too painful. It was simply that the other captives talked about nothing but their potential mates. They complained and whined about their captivity, but they also talked about the males. This one was so sweet, they were all so big and strong, and that one had such pretty eyes. The females wondered who they would match and what would happen once the men found out which female was capable of giving them offspring.

Since their arrival on this planet, the males had focused on creating the actual settlement. They'd cleared large sections of land for shuttle lots, training fields, and the multi-ship complex that now housed five of the six thousand occupants. The overlord had also forbidden his men from being alone with any of the females. The females were required to travel in small groups whenever they left the security of their cabins. Until Overlord Razel deemed the compound safe, the physical pleasure of his men would have to wait.

"Can I help you with something, ladies?"

The deep, indolent voice made Lily whip her head toward the speaker. He lounged in the hatchway, arms crossed over his chest. Long dark hair framed his handsome face and flowed in wide waves past his shoulders. He wasn't as tall as many of the Rodytes and his body appeared lean rather than bulkily muscular. He wore brown pants that looked as if they'd been braided out of leather strips and a snug green shirt rather than the khaki uniforms favored by most of the Outcasts. He also had a neatly trimmed beard, which was unusual for a Rodyte. A cluster of braids at his temple had been decorated with metal beads. Lily had seen him before, but she didn't know his name.

"We were just..." Unable to manufacture a believable lie, Lily just shrugged helplessly.

Thea moved forward, her steps calculative. She tossed back her long blonde hair as a wily gleam brightened her dark eyes. "Are you Rex Dravon?"

"Who wants to know?" His tone turned silky and he moved toward Thea, his stride lazy and rolling.

"I'm Wilma. She's Betty."

Though Thea's tone had been conversational, the male laughed. "Does that make me Fred or Barney?"

Thea shot her a surprised glance before admitting, "I didn't expect you to understand the reference."

"I'm aware."

Completely derailed by his reaction, Thea struggled to recover control of the situation. "You didn't answer my question."

"Neither did you," he pointed out. "At least, not honestly. Shall we start over? I'm Rex Dravon. And you are?"

"Thea Cline. You are just as attractive as I'd heard." Her flirtatiousness gradually returned. Lily had seen the strategy at work before. Thea flattered and teased, subtly extracting information with carefully veiled questions. "I know you work with the Outcasts, but do you consider yourself one of them?"

"Ahh." He glanced at Lily, clearly seeing right through the attempt. "You're looking for a ride off this rock."

Thea didn't deny it. "Wouldn't you?"

"Probably." He sauntered forward, closing the distance between him and Thea. It didn't take much. The shuttle was tiny. He rested one palm against the fuselage and leaned down slightly, mimicking her slightly seductive tone. "Problem is, even if I don't consider myself an Outcast, they're my only customer at the moment. If I piss off the overlord, I shut down a very lucrative revenue stream."

"Some things are more important than money." Thea met his gaze directly, chin raised stubbornly. "Take us to safety and we'll pay you whatever you ask."

His dark gaze swept down her body, then back to her face. "Tempting, but I can buy all the pleasure givers I want with what Kage pays me."

"That's not what I meant," she stressed. "Name your price and we'll meet it. 'Kage' doesn't need to know how we escaped."

"He'd know. Overlord Razel has a pet harbinger who keeps him informed about anything that affects the Outcasts."

Just the mention of the harbinger made Lily tense. Arton the Heretic, the overlord's "pet harbinger" was a thorn in Lily's side. Reported to have powerful psychic abilities, Arton only spoke when he had something important to say. Except when he was around Lily. He harassed her on a daily basis, attempting to convince her to unlock the datapad they'd stolen from her supervisor, or provide them with the chemical formula needed to stabilize the genetic transformation each couple would need to undergo. Without the formula, the Outcasts' breeding program was dead in the water.

Most of the Outcasts had been born with latent magic, but Rodyte scientists found a way to unleash that power during the mating process. When a Rodyte male claimed his mate, it triggered a mutual metamorphosis that increased the chances of conception. By using this natural transformation as a delivery mechanism, the scientists were able to insert genetic modifications without either body rejecting the changes.

Lily had been working with the Rodyte doctor who supervised the transformation project back on Earth and the Outcasts desperately needed her expertise if they were to launch a transformation program of their own. She wasn't sure why the overlord had chosen Arton as her tormentor, but he seemed to enjoy the assignment. Fortunately, for Lily, her stubborn nature had kept him from succeeding. So far.

"You have no problem with their kidnapping us and dragging us to this godforsaken wilderness?"

If Thea was trying to shame Rex Dravon into helping them, Lily was pretty sure she was wasting her time. Lily was well acquainted with his reputation. She just hadn't known what he looked like until now. According to all the gossip, he was a ruthless smuggler who only cared about money. He'd admitted as much a few minutes ago.

He lifted one broad shoulder in a halfhearted shrug. He was a handsome devil as Thea had said. Way too many of the Outcasts were. "I see both sides of most arguments. You don't like losing control and they just want to survive."

"And you're just trying to make a buck?" Thea made the possibility sound cowardly.

Rex laughed. "I'm a businessman. There's nothing shameful in focusing on prosperity."

"There is if people are being harmed in the process!"

"You look pretty hale and hearty to me." Something dangerous gleamed in his gaze as the smile faded from his lips. Like most Rodytes, his eyes were so dark they appeared black, and the gold rings, known as phitons, gleamed hypnotically. "I've seen abused prisoners, sweetheart. Neither of you qualify."

"So the trap worked."

The amusement in Arton's now familiar voice snapped Lily's head back toward the hatchway. The harbinger stood there, much as Rex had earlier. Arton was taller than Rex and more muscular. With Arton, it was his coloring that set him apart from other Rodytes. His hair was a unique combination of silver and black.

His strange gray-blue gaze settled on Lily. "I would have been surprised if Thea hadn't taken the bait, but I expected better from you."

"Bait for what?" Thea asked before Lily could respond. "What was the purpose for your 'trap'?"

"It had been ten days since the last escape attempt. We were considering rolling back some of the restrictions. Obviously, that won't happen now."

"We weren't trying to escape," Lily insisted, not wanting the others to suffer for her misbehavior.

His brows arched and his phitons gleamed like polished silver. "Really? Then what are you doing on this shuttle?"

"Looking for weapons." She glared into his eyes. There was something about this male that made her feisty. "We're stuck on this planet whether we like it or not. We didn't want to be defenseless."

Without changing his expression he reached down and unclasped the blaster strapped to his thigh. After checking a setting on the weapon's side, he handed it to her. It felt cold and heavy in her hand, so she immediately lowered it to point at the floor. She'd never learned how to shoot a gun and had no interest in learning now.

"Do you feel safer now?" he challenged.

His sarcasm annoyed her, made her want to lash out. "You're right, I'm unlikely to shoot you, but we both know she won't hesitate." She handed the blaster to Thea, who immediately aimed it at his face.

"This is *not* happening on my shuttle." Rex quickly took the gun from Thea and handed it back to the harbinger. Then he looked at Thea again, humor making his dark eyes shine. "You blast his brains all over the walls, baby doll, and I'm the one who has to clean it up."

Baby doll? Thea ignored the nickname. In fact she looked as if she intended to pretend the smuggler had ceased to exist.

"Thanks for your help, Rex," Arton said as he reached for Lily's arm. "Someone will be along to collect her in a few minutes." He nodded toward Thea as he drew Lily toward the hatch.

"No thank you." Lily twisted out of his light hold. "Thea is one of my roommates. The guards can escort us both. Females are not supposed to be alone with any of you."

"She has a point." Rex was clearly enjoying the conflict.

Without responding to the provocation, Arton focused entirely on Lily. "Thea is going to detention. You're coming with me." He offered no other information.

Lily dug in her heels, feeling restless and oddly achy. "If this is a punishable offence, I should go to detention too."

"Maybe later." His long fingers wrapped around her upper arm with steely efficiency. He wasn't hurting her, but all the tugging in the world wouldn't set her free.

They descended the stairs and emerged in the sunlit meadow. Left with no other choice, Lily rushed along beside him, struggling to keep up with his long-legged strides. The shuttles blurred and her shoes skid across the thick turquois grass as she focused on her tormentor. He wore blue jeans and a black T-shirt with a brewery's logo on the front. Earth garments would have been welcomed by the captives, but they'd been forced to wear the same ugly khaki uniforms as most of the Outcasts. Apparently, the overlord's pet harbinger wasn't subject to any of the rules.

She wasn't surprised. Not only was Arton a powerful psychic, he was second-in-command of the Outcasts. Arton answered to Overlord Razel, and only Razel. She'd seen him break up fights and berate seasoned warriors who immediately responded with deference and respect. The rank-and-file Outcasts genuinely liked their overlord, but they feared the heretic.

"Where are you taking me?" She cringed at the shrillness in her tone. She didn't want him to realize how fast her heart was beating. Each of their arguments had become more volatile and the tension pulsing between them was already palpable.

"Somewhere without distractions." He didn't turn his head, didn't slow his pace, just hurried along, dragging her behind him.

"What the hell is that supposed to mean?" And why did Arton piss her off faster than any person she'd ever met? Yes, he was intentionally provocative, but her easygoing nature vanished the second he walked into a room. "Distractions from what?"

He stopped and pivoted toward her, his gaze boring into hers. "You know damn well what you're supposed to be doing and it has nothing to do with stealing weapons."

"Not this again." She rolled her eyes and stared off into the distance. "Aren't you tired of the same old argument?"

"Extremely. That's why it ends today." Without explaining that ominous statement, he resumed his discourteous pace.

She continued glaring at him. Not that he noticed. His face remained forward, gaze fixed straight ahead. He drew her into the trees surrounding the shuttle lot. The shadows hadn't felt this cool or threatening while she explored with Thea. If Arton wanted to hurt her, he'd had plenty of opportunities. Most of their arguments had taken place in corridors, but other captives had been nearby. She was truly alone with him for the first time and it made him seem larger and more menacing.

When it became obvious that Arton wouldn't leave Lily alone, she decided to do some research. Knowledge was power and she had always thought it wise to know as much as possible about her enemies. Rumors and speculation ran rampant about harbingers in general, and Arton in particular, on both the battle born ships to which she'd been assigned. Both ships had been commanded by Arton's younger brothers, or half-brothers. They all shared a father, Kryton Lux, a retired general who still held sway with Rodymia's ruling class. Arton was born to Kryton's first lifemate, while the younger three Lux brothers were born to Skyla, Kryton's current mate, and the love of his life. Because of Lily's interaction with Arton's brothers, she knew a fair amount about his family. Arton personally, however, was still very much a mystery.

To participate in the transformation program, each male was required to fill out a detailed profile. When Lily checked the database, she discovered that Arton didn't have a profile. Apparently, he wasn't interested in a mate.

Lily refused to analyze the emotions that discovery unleashed. Was it possible he wanted a mate but didn't care about—or wasn't capable of producing—children? Either way it made no difference to her. She was certainly not interested in bonding with any Rodyte, especially one as disagreeable as Arton.

The setback in her investigation disappointed Lily, but she didn't give up. She wasn't able to find information on Arton personally. Still, she found all sorts of articles, news reports and interviews pertaining to harbingers in general. Their abilities were the unintended result of genetic engineering. The mutation that gave them their psychic powers also produced their unique coloring. Anything involving harbingers was controlled by their powerful guild leaders. The guild owned and operated the fortress-like academy and was responsible for the aggressive recruitment policies. Most infants born with harbinger coloring were taken to Harbinger Academy voluntarily so they could be educated and trained by other empowered Rodytes. If the family refused to relinquish their child, however, the baby was taken by force.

Lily shivered. Had Arton been torn from a loving family? Was that why she frequently saw pain and hatred in his eyes? She knew he had no contact with his brothers or his parents, but she didn't know the reason for the estrangement.

It didn't matter. She couldn't let it matter. She alone could protect the other captives, and maybe someday find a way to return them to Earth. "You know I can't help you and you know why. Do we have to keep having this conversation?" She forced calm into her voice, hoping to deescalate the tension.

"You were helping the battle born," he reminded. "Why do you find us less worthy than them?"

Guilt panged through her soul in response to the accusation in his deep tone. Technically most of the Outcast were battle born. Their mothers were Bilarrian prisoners forced to breed with their Rodyte captors. It had been the males' hope that their offspring would "restore" magic to the Rodyte people. Lily found the practice horrific, but refused to blame the sons for the sins of their fathers. Despite their unconventional parentage, the battle born were determined to leave the past behind and claim a future free from subjugation and prejudice.

The Outcasts, on the other hand, emulated their fathers, taking what they wanted without mercy or regret. "The battle born *asked* for my help. They didn't kidnap me and hold me against my will."

He scoffed, still not bothering to look at her. "They brought an army to Earth and surrounded the planet with spaceships. Your people only offered to help them because they knew there was no other choice."

"That's not true. The battle born forced nothing on Earth. In fact they defended us against other alien invaders."

He looked down at her then, his expression inscrutable. "Are you really that naïve? The battle born are every bit as ruthless as the Outcasts. They just use manipulation and intimidation to get what they want. We're less hypocritical."

They could debate the past for the rest of their lives and it wouldn't change the present situation. "Your opinion of the battle born is irrelevant. I will not help you force your will on human females."

"What if they volunteer?"

They reached the other side of the woods separating the shuttle lot from the multi-ship compound. Twelve identical ships had been positioned with their narrow bows pointed inward and their wide stern sections outward. The ships were then connected by airlocks and railed walkways, forming a massive pizza-shaped complex that enabled the Outcasts to consolidate resources and better defend their new home. All of the females and about half the males were now housed aboard the "Wheel". The other thousand males had been dispersed through the remaining ships, so they could perform security sweeps, as well as hunting and scouting expeditions. The secluded location of the planet made supply runs time-consuming and expensive. The hope was for the settlement to become as self-sustaining as possible.

"What are you talking about?" she asked. He released her arm as they reached the zigzagging gangplank leading up to *Viper*, ship eight in the Wheel. It was the ship on which Lily, Thea, and their other two roommates had traveled from Earth. The overlord and his entourage had moved their lodgings to the *Viper* shortly after their arrival, so it was now a sort of headquarters for the Outcasts.

The walkway was narrow enough that they couldn't walk side by side. There was a wider, less steep entry ramp on the other side of the ship that led to common areas like dining halls and the workout center. This ramp took them directly to deck three where the majority of the females were assigned. Their apparent destination helped Lily relax and not sound so confrontational. "How can a captive 'volunteer' for anything?"

"You're no longer captives. You're allowed to go anywhere you like."

"Except back to Earth," she snapped, annoyed by his nonchalance. "We're all here against our will. Until that changes, everything else is moot."

She paused for a moment on the landing at the top of the gangplank. Their elevated position allowed her to see over the treetops. Miles and miles of forest spread out to the east, the undulating field of turquoise broken only by the areas the Outcasts had cleared. To the west a massive body of water gleamed like emerald glass. Fluffy clouds partially blocked the sun, but another object hung in the sky unobstructed, almost intrusive.

"Did you guys give it a name?" She pointed toward the large planet clearly visible above their heads. Like the blue-green leaves, it was a constant reminder that she was no longer on Earth.

"The team of scientists that first explored this area named it Scarlett." Much of the planet appeared red, so Lily didn't question the name. Then he added, "They call this planet Rhett."

The combination made her smile. "Do you understand the reference?"

"I didn't at the time, but I have since read portions of the book and watched scenes from the motion picture."

She accepted his answer with a nod. The Outcasts' knowledge of Earth frequently surprised her. On the surface they appeared to be brutal warriors only concerned with warfare. This was one of many examples proving there was more to these men than their militant appearance. "How did a team of Rodyte scientists learn about *Gone with the Wind*?"

"Humans hold the key to our survival. We've all been learning as much as we can about your various cultures."

The key to their survival? Was that how they saw their captive brides? How they justified the mass kidnapping? She knew from working with the battle born that the Rodyte race was in trouble. They'd been altering their DNA for so long that unexpected complications were now common. Genetic compatibility between pureblooded Rodytes was rare, and hybrid matches were even more infrequent. That was why they'd searched for other humanoid races capable of producing offspring with Rodytes. And their desperate search led them to Earth.

The ship felt closed, almost claustrophobic after hours in the fresh air. Each corridor was rounded, more like a tunnel than a hallway. The decks were coarsely textured for added traction while the matte-gray walls were smooth. Arton reached the forward lift and motioned her inside.

Tension returned with a vengeance. "My cabin is down there." She indicated the other end of the rounded corridor.

"I know." An enigmatic smile lifted one corner of his mouth. "We're going to mine." The silver rings in his smoky eyes shimmered, but his expression revealed only his determination to be obeyed. "You can walk or I'll carry you. The choice is yours."

She looked up and down the corridor, deciding if she gained anything by refusing. He was at least eight inches taller than her and close to twice her weight. A physical confrontation would be no contest. "Why are we going to your cabin?"

Rather than argue with her, he leaned down and swept her into his arms, cradling her against his chest like a child.

She gasped and instinctively wrapped her arm around his neck. At least he hadn't slung her facedown over his shoulder. "The argument doesn't change if you lock me in your cabin."

Their faces were on a level as he carried her into the lift, which focused her gaze on his sculpted features. Strong yet noble, his face reminded her of the armored angels so popular in Renaissance art. But the rest of him was anything but angelic. His biceps were so thick they strained the sleeves of his T-shirt and his forearms were covered in the Rodyte equivalent of tattoos. His muscular body emanated raw power and defiance blazed in his silver-ringed eyes. How was she supposed to win any confrontation with Arton the Heretic?

Arton stared into Lily's vivid blue eyes and his thoughts scattered. He wanted to kiss her, feel her lips part beneath his and taste the sweetness of her mouth. With silky black hair and porcelain skin, she'd attracted him the first time he saw her. But he was not looking for a mate, and Lily deserved more than a few heated encounters with no long-term commitment. If the others detected his scent on her, it would indicate that she was willing to share pleasure without being claimed. Regardless of how appealing he found her, he would not help turn Lily into a pleasure giver. Such was frequently the fate for unprotected females.

"No distractions," he reminded, forcing his thoughts away from her soft-looking lips. Her unique appearance had made him curious enough to ask Kage about possible causes. The overlord knew more about Earth than most of his men. According to Kage, the exotic shape of her eyes and the sculpted contours of her face were the result of an Asian parent. Her vivid blue eyes, however, indicated that her other parent was likely European. Arton found the combination enchanting. "We're going to talk this out without interruptions." Then he needed to set her down as soon as possible, because being this close to her, feeling her softness press against him, drove all thoughts of negotiation from his mind.

They reached deck four and he exited the lift, then carefully placed her on her feet. She immediately stepped back, taking her body just out of reach.

"What can you say to me that you haven't said ten times before?" She looked back at the lift as if she'd try to run, but ultimately fell into step beside him.

"Actually, there have been some developments of which you're not yet aware. I'm hoping they will change your outlook on the situation." They turned a corner and entered the short hallway leading to the officer cabins. As they approached his door, the privacy panel directly across from his opened.

Kage Razel stood framed by the threshold, his dark head nearly touching the lintel. His outfit caught Arton by surprise. Kage had abandoned the "barbarian" costume he wore to intimidate those interested in hiring the Outcasts or those foolish enough to compete for the same contracts. For the past few weeks he'd worn a nondescript uniform just like his men. At the moment, he was bare to the waist except for the munitions harness crisscrossing his broad chest. He wore synthleather pants and knee-high boots. His head had been recently shaved on the sides, but a narrow section of long hair ran from front to back down the middle of his head. Much of his torso and both arms were covered with detailed images and raised sigils, commemorating events or expressing meaning only Kage understood.

"Overlord," Arton greeted, glancing at Lily to gauge her reaction to his best friend.

Her eyes were wide and her mouth hung open for just a moment before she snapped it shut. She moved closer to Arton, but he was relatively sure it hadn't been a conscious decision. Kage had that effect on a lot of people. His size alone was enough to intimidate.

"Have you told her yet?" Kage asked without preamble.

"I was about to."

Displeasure narrowed Kage's dark eyes. "It's been at least an hour since I told you to find her. Where have you been?"

"On Rex's shuttle. Two intrepid females took the bait."

"Lily was one?" Kage looked at her, his scowl giving way to disbelief.

"Surprised me too."

"Who was the other?" He didn't give Arton time to respond. "Never mind. It had to be Thea. I never should have left them in the same cabin. Thea must be claimed as soon as possible. That woman is a menace."

"You can't be serious." Despite Lily's fear, she came alive in defense of her friend. "It's only been a few months since she lost her husband and children. She might never tolerate another male. She's certainly not ready now."

Kage waved away her concerns. "She has six matches. One of them will be able to overcome her painful past. You need to focus on the problem at hand. You both do." Kage shot him a look that warned him not to argue. "I thought of a way to speed up the negotiations."

"There is nothing to negotiate," Lily objected, her voice soft but tense. "The only thing we want is our freedom and you aren't willing to—"

Kage took her hand and snapped a tether band around her wrist before she could finish her argument.

"What the hell is this?" She held up her arm now encircled by the smooth alloy band.

"It creates an electronic tether," Arton told her. Then he looked at Kage and asked, "What are the parameters?"

"Ten feet." Kage accented the revelation with a humorless smile, then he motioned toward Arton's arm. "At least I allowed barriers."

His gaze narrowed and he clasped his hands behind his back. "Make it twenty-five."

"She's not the only one who needs motivation."

"Ten feet is impossible," Arton argued. They would have to sleep in the same room. There was more than ten feet between his bed and the couch in his living room.

Kage motioned toward Arton's arm again, but he ignored the gesture. "If you'd been more persuasive, this wouldn't be necessary."

"Lengthen the tether and I'll consider it."

Any hint of humor evaporated and Kage's dark eyes turned cold. "I didn't ask for your input. Hold out your arm. That's an order."

When the overlord gave a direct order, even his best friend was expected to obey. Resenting the situation more with every passing second, Arton slowly unclasped his hands and held out his arm. The band snapped into place and automatically connected, forming a seal only Kage could deactivate.

"You have until morning." Kage's icy tone echoed his expression. "This is your last chance. Make her see reason, or we move forward without her." He stepped back and the privacy panel slid shut.

Arton looked at Lily. Had she heard the ultimatum?

Her attention appeared to be focused entirely on the band. She ran her fingers along every surface, searching for a release. When she found none, she tugged with all her might, trying to slip her hand free. "What happens if we get more than ten feet from each other?"

"It triggers the pain center of your brain," he told her. "Trust me. You don't want to feel the result."

Her expressive blue gaze shifted from her arm to his face. "You've heard or you know from experience?"

This was the closest they'd ever come to a normal conversation. Had this mutual insult finally given them a common ground? He glanced at Kage's door. The wily bastard probably planned it that way.

Arton scanned open his cabin and motioned her inside before answering her question. "I was tethered to a string of instructors until I turned twelve."

She took two steps into the cabin, but went no farther. "What happened then?"

He seldom thought about his years at Harbinger Academy and never spoke about the abuse he'd endured. But there was too much at stake for him to hide behind his pride. If he could transform her curiosity into cooperation, a few unpleasant memories would be well worth it. "Like you, I accepted that escape was impossible."

"I haven't accepted anything," she warned.

Brushing past her, he walked farther into the room, hoping she'd follow. She didn't. "Kage doesn't make idle threats. If you don't agree to cooperate, he will move on without you in the morning."

Concern flickered through her gaze, yet her other features remained impassive. "Move on without me?" Challenge threaded through her tone. She still believed she had the upper hand. "That's not possible. The transformation cannot be stabilized without the formula. If the overlord tries, people will die."

"We're well aware." Arton moved to the sofa and sat, refusing to give in to her stubbornness. If she wanted to stand over there by the door, let her. This was doubtlessly going to be a long, frustrating conversation. "Fortunately for us, you're not the only geneticist in this star system. Our team is relatively sure they've replicated the formula."

A tall-backed armchair faced the sofa. She moved to stand behind it and rested her hands on top of the back cushion. "'Relatively sure?'" Her challenging tone sharpened. "He's willing to risk lives on 'relatively sure'?"

"So audit their formula." He crossed his legs and pressed back into the sofa, his voice every bit as challenging as hers. "Tell me where they went wrong or if they got it right."

"If it's wrong, I won't tell you how to fix it," she warned.

He chuckled. "Then you'll tell me it's wrong even if it's right. I'm not stupid, Lily. But this has to end." He uncrossed his legs and scooted to the edge of the sofa. "I'm asking you to help me prevent Kage from doing something rash. We've been here a month and the men are dangerously restless. If he doesn't launch the transformation program soon, someone will challenge his right to rule."

She finger-combed her hair back from her face as she worried her bottom lip. "Let me see it." She sounded annoyed by her own request.

Pushing to his feet, he crossed the room and picked up his datapad. The formula was already on the screen. He'd been looking at it when Rex notified him that a couple of females had sneaked onto his shuttle. "Translate using human equivalents," he instructed the handheld computer. Once the translation was complete, he crossed the room and handed her the device.

She studied the complex formula for a moment then shook her head. "It's surprisingly close, but there are two mistakes. They cannot attempt a transformation with this formula. The result would be uncertain at best."

He searched her gaze. She stared back at him, her expression open and seemingly honest. "Damn it," he muttered. "I can't tell if you're lying or not."

"I'm not," she insisted. "This formula is flawed."

"Then fix it. The program launches tomorrow with this formula unless you fix it."

"You must convince them to wait." She set the datapad down on a nearby table. "Even if the formula is right, the result is still at risk. The transformation cannot be forced. Resistance on the part of either party adversely affects the outcome."

Seeing the uncertainty in her eyes, he advanced. Kage was right. Arton hadn't been nearly as persuasive as he was capable of being. He hadn't wanted to frighten her. Well, the time for diplomacy was past. He either convinced Lily to help them or lives could be lost. "The couple came to us. They both want this badly."

She echoed his movements, retreating as he advanced, until her back pressed against the bulkhead. "I don't believe you."

"He was assigned to guard your section, so they were together every day. Others commented on their attraction. Did you honestly not notice?"

"Oh no." Her hand flew to her throat and color bled from her lovely face. "You're talking about Jillian and Stront."

He nodded. "Stront suspected that they were compatible, so Kage saw no reason not to tell him. Not only is Jillian his potential mate, but she has no other matches."

Lily shook her head, eyes wide with fear. "You can't let them do this. The results could be disastrous."

"Then fix it!" He slapped his hand against the bulkhead and leaned in, his nose nearly touching hers. "Their lives are in your hands."

Chapter Two

L ily's throat tensed as her heart pounded in her chest. She could feel Arton's breath on her lips, warm and inviting. For one mad instant, she wanted him to kiss her, longed to lose herself in passion and wish the conflicts of this strange world far away. But lives were at stake and Arton wasn't interested in her as a woman, just as a scientist. She shook her head, snapping reality back into place.

"I won't be bullied," she said firmly. "If Stront wants to risk his life, that's between him and the overlord. But I want to talk to Jillian. Take me back to my cabin."

"No." He moved his other hand to the bulkhead, surrounding her with his body. "If you want to protect your friend, fix the formula."

Raising both hands to his chest, she shoved with all her might. He wouldn't budge and the contact only accented his nearness, made her feel trapped and...tingly. She tried to duck under his arm. He caught her upper arms and pressed her back into place.

"Even if I let you go to her, it wouldn't matter." His tone deepened and his gaze began to smolder. "She's experiencing the pull." He bent and pressed his face against her hair, inhaling deeply. "Do you know what that means?"

She held perfectly still. He was scenting her, absorbing her pheromones to see if his body reacted. She knew all about the pull. The workstation in each cabin had been activated, though the access was limited. The captives could read books, trigger entertainment files, and detailed information about the transformation program. That was how the females explored the profiles of eligible males. The list of matches hadn't been released yet, but Stront and Jillian weren't the only compatible couple to find each other on their own.

"I know what it means." She finally responded to his nearly forgotten question. "Instincts—and body chemistry—draw compatible couples together and urge them to...procreate. The level of compatibility determines the strength of their urges." Did that explain her fascination with Arton? The pull wouldn't kick in until he kissed her, but often females had a vague sense that something was different about a potential mate even before they kissed. She'd attributed her interest in Arton to the mystique surrounding his abilities. She'd never met a bonafide psychic before, much less one laser focused on her.

He raised one hand and stroked the side of her face, then gently tilted her head back. Excitement and fear twisted through her and she shook her head. If he kissed her, and if they were compatible, his taste would activate the pull in her. She wasn't ready for this, wasn't sure she wanted to find out she was genetically compatible with an alien. But he didn't kiss her. He turned her head to the side and pressed his face against her throat.

"We're not compatible," he whispered. "So why do you smell so damn good?"

She tensed, yet disappointment washed over her in sobering waves. "How do you know if we're compatible or not? You're not in the database of eligible males. Did you have our DNA tested on your own?"

A chuckle rumbled through his chest and his lips brushed against the sensitive skin on the side of her neck. Tingles spread out across her flesh and she shivered. Why was he still touching her if they weren't potential mates? And why in the world was she disappointed about his revelation?

He lifted his head and looked into her eyes. "Were you researching me?"

She shrugged, feeling anything but indifferent. In four short weeks many of the captives had begun to accept their new reality. They no longer thought about Earth and all they'd left behind. Instead they dreamed of the male who would claim them and anticipated a future on this untamed planet. It was hard not to become swept up in their excitement when she was continually surrounded by it. "It's basic strategy to know as much as you can about your enemy."

"Are we enemies?" He feathered kisses along her jawline, moving up toward her ear. "I don't hate you. Do you hate me?"

He sucked her earlobe into his mouth and all she could do was gasp. The simple contact launched sensation in multiple directions. Tingles branched out across the back of her head while heat spiraled deep into her abdomen. Her nipples tingled and her core ached, responding despite all her mind's logical objections.

"I need your help, Lily." He whispered the words into her ear as he brushed her cheek with his knuckles. "Protect Jillian."

His thumb stroked over her lips. "Protect all the females. Keep them safe as they settle into their new lives."

She narrowed her gaze on his handsome face, recovering enough to recognize his tactic. "I'm not desperate enough to fall for this shit. Stop touching me!" She batted his hand aside and tried again to push him away.

He wrapped his arm around her waist and pulled her forward, pressing her body against his from chest to knees. "I'm not sure I can. I've never felt this way before."

Acting on instinct, she drew back her arm and slapped him hard across the face. His head snapped to the side, then he struck like a snake. He grabbed both her wrists and pinned them to the bulkhead on either side of her head. His jaw clenched and fury flashed through his silver-ringed eyes.

"Now you're pissed off," she pointed out. "Surely you've felt *that* way before."

Understanding slowly penetrated his anger and he finally released her. He lowered his arms and reluctantly stepped back. "Hit me again and there will be consequences."

He was right. She shouldn't have hit him. That was just as wrong as him attempting to seduce her. She was smart enough to resolve conflicts without resorting to violence. "I want to talk to Jillian." She crossed her arms over her chest, hoping he wouldn't notice her beaded nipples. It was irrational to want someone she didn't even like.

"It won't make a difference," he predicted, slipping back behind the brooding mask he wore so often.

"Then what do you have to lose? Don't I have until morning to make up my mind?"

He raked his hair with one hand, jaw still tight, nostrils flared. "If Jillian changes her mind, Kage will simply find another couple. Your friend isn't the only female who has already been contacted by her potential mate. In fact couples are being drawn together so fast, we might not need to use the database."

"I still want to talk to her." Nothing spread faster than gossip. If she detailed her concerns with Jillian and Sara, they would doubtlessly warn the other females. Even if her warnings didn't keep all the women from falling under the Outcasts' spell, she might make them leery enough to slow things down until she figured out another course of action.

"If you aren't able to convince her to withdraw, will you fix the formula?"

She glared at him. This was so unfair. She was damned either way. If she fixed the formula, she was assisting the Outcasts in carrying out their twisted plan. But if she refused to correct their mistakes, Jillian—or one of the others—would likely be harmed, perhaps killed by the resulting transformation.

She had to do something. "I'll decide after I've spoken with her."

With a frustrated sigh, he relented. "Fine. Let's go."

He escorted her to the cabin she shared with the other three females. With bunkbeds, a corner workstation, and one tiny bathroom, there wasn't much to recommend the accommodations. She scanned open the door and was pleasantly surprised when Arton remained in the corridor as she stepped inside.

"Oh thank God!" Sara cried, quickly climbing down from her top bunk so she could give Lily a hug.

"We heard you and Thea had been arrested," Jillian explained. She sat cross-legged on the middle of the bunk beneath Sara's. "Did you really try to steal a shuttle?"

Sara moved aside, so Lily sat on the foot of Jillian's bunk. At twenty-three, Jillian was the youngest of the four roommates, and her freckled complexion made her appear even younger. She had short blonde hair, baby-blue eyes, and a smile that lit up her face. Lily, and even more so Thea, felt very protective of the younger woman. Jillian's naiveté was the primary reason they'd both been so concerned when her attraction to Stront became obvious.

"We were looking for weapons, not trying to escape," Lily told them, "but the result was the same. Thea's down in detention and I'm now tethered to the harbinger." She held up her wrist, displaying the alien bracelet. "If I get too far away from him, it zaps me."

"How long is your leash?" Sara wanted to know. She was a pretty Latina with long dark hair and even darker eyes.

"Ten feet. He's out in the hallway."

"What are they going to do to Thea?" Sara digressed, worry creasing he bow.

"They're hoping her mate will settle her down," Lily grumbled, unable to hide her dislike of the idea.

Jillian scoffed. "They obviously don't know Thea. Any man that tries to control her will have a wildcat on his hands." Admiration made her words sound almost wistful.

"It's only been a few months since she lost her whole family." Sara shook her head, clearly upset by the suggestion. "How can they expect her to... It's just not right."

"Who knows." Jillian scooted back and leaned against the bulkhead. "A loving man could be exactly what she needs."

Lily hadn't been sure how to bring up the transformation program, but Jillian had just given her an opening. "Is a loving man exactly what you need? I thought we'd all agreed to defy them."

Jillian stilled. Her thick-lashed gaze darted toward Sara, then returned to Lily's face. "Stront is different than any man I've ever met."

"Could be because he's not a man at all," Sara chimed in, disapproval clear in her dark eyes. "He's an alien, an alien that kidnapped you and is holding you against your will."

"Is it still 'against your will'?" Lily challenged. "Did you honestly volunteer to go first?"

Sara gasped. "She did what?"

"Stront and Jillian went to the overlord and asked if they could go first." Lily shifted her gaze back to Jillian, who had drawn her legs up in front of her and was refusing to look at either Sara or her. "Did Stront put you up to it, or was it your idea?"

Her only response was a one-shouldered shrug.

"Have you had sex with him?" Sara's question sounded more like an accusation.

"By Bill Clinton's definition of sex or my mother's?" A faint smile quirked the corners of Jillian's mouth.

Lily didn't even want to know the distinction. "Sexual contact of *any kind* will make the cravings stronger."

She finally looked up. "Yeah, we figured that out. If Stront doesn't claim me soon, we'll both go insane!"

"I can't believe this." Sara tossed back her long dark hair, too agitated to stand still. "Did you not hear one word Lily told us? Transformation is dangerous under the best of circumstances. The Outcasts don't even know what the hell they're doing."

"That's not true!" Jillian unfolded her legs and swung her feet to the floor, apparently ready for a verbal battle. "We met with Dr. Foran. He answered all of our questions, so he has to be familiar with the process."

"Did you ask him how many transformations he has overseen?" Lily challenged. "To my knowledge, the only successful transformations took place on battle born ships, so I'm relatively sure the answer is zero."

Jillian's shrug was slightly more convincing this time. "Someone has to go first. It might as well be me."

"That's so ignorant." Sara turned her back. "I can't even look at you right now."

Lily tried not to smile, but failed. Sara was passionate about everything. She was also loving and often selfless, which made her volatility easier to tolerate. Challenging Jillian directly was only making her more determined, so Lily changed strategy. She pushed to her feet and let confusion fill her tone. "I thought you loved him."

"Of course I love him." She sounded horribly affronted. "Why would you say that?"

"If you love him, why are you encouraging him to do something that will likely cause him harm, maybe even end his life?"

Jillian's mouth opened then closed. She licked her lips, then squared her shoulders. "If it's so dangerous and Dr. Foran is so incompetent, why don't you direct the program? That's why they brought you along."

"They didn't just bring me along," Lily snapped, but the barb found its mark. Not being compatible with anyone was especially annoying after Arton's careless comment about the same damn thing.

Jillian's tone softened and regret sparked in her big blue eyes. "I didn't mean it like that. You know how the transformation works and you've overseen many of them. Why won't you help us?"

"'Help *us*'?" Sara spun back around, eyes wide with disbelief. "You're siding with the Outcasts now?"

Lily had reacted similarly. Sara just beat her to the reply. Jillian didn't respond, so Lily tried to drive her point home. "If I help them now, it puts us all in danger. Are you really selfish enough to make this decision for everyone?"

Jillian shook her head, her gaze defiant again. "It doesn't work that way. The transformation can't be forced. Dr. Foran said the result is always flawed if there is any sort of resistance. Every female has to choose for themselves."

"Every female will be ruthlessly seduced by a male whose kiss is a sexual stimulant," Lily argued.

"The pull only amplifies attraction. It doesn't create it," Jillian stressed, obviously anther quote from the Rodyte doctor. "It won't kick in unless the woman wants the male just as much. It can't be one-sided." She paused and shook her head. "You make it sound like a date rape drug."

"*Dios*, you sound like one of them." Sara glared at the younger woman, anger blazing in her dark eyes.

"It might not be a date rape drug, but it clouds the mind and warps priorities," Lily argued.

"So does alcohol," Jillian persisted. "And they still serve alcohol at weddings."

Lily ignored the outburst and stayed focused on the situation at hand. "All that matters to you right now is being with Stront. You're not thinking clearly."

This time Jillian hesitated before she responded. "I'm doing this with or without you. Obviously, I would much rather have you involved."

"I hope to God you don't mean that, because I cannot give in to them."

"You *won't* give in because you're stubborn and filled with pride."

"Jillian!" Sara's voice went up an octave and she put both hands on her hips. "That's hateful. Apologize right now."

"No. You guys treat me like a child, but I'm not. I'm not even a virgin. I'm in love with Stront and I want him to claim me so he'll have access to his magic." If Jillian had realized how childish this made her sound, she might have chosen her words more carefully.

"There's no guarantee that will happen," Lily reminded. "About thirty percent of the couples I dealt with didn't end up with abilities of any kind."

"Which mean seventy percent unleashed their magic." Jillian's chin lifted. "I'll take those odds."

"Those are the odds with my formula," Lily stressed. "That's not what they'll be using in the morning."

"It's not just me, you know." Jillian squared her shoulders and stared into Lily's eyes. "If we took a vote right now, asked everyone what they wanted you to do, my side would win by a landslide."

"Even if they knew they'd be risking their lives?" Lily countered.

Jillian's gaze narrowed and her lips pressed into an angry line. "You'll really let me die just so you don't have to 'give in to them'?"

"I won't do anything. What happens tomorrow is entirely up to you, but I *will not* give my formula to kidnappers and criminals." Angry and frustrated, Lily rushed from the room.

Arton stood in the corridor, arms crossed over his broad chest. He was trying to hide his smile, but the corners of his mouth kept twitching. He couldn't hear the conversation going on inside the tiny cabin, but he could easily imagine the exchange. Females in the grip of the pull rarely changed their minds about wanting their mate. The pull was instinctual and intense. Rather like his attraction to Lily. But they weren't compatible, so why did he want her so badly?

The privacy panel slid open and Lily stormed out. "You knew that would happen, didn't you?"

He pushed off the wall and fell into step beside her. "I had a pretty good idea it would be a waste of time." Her only response was a tense shake of her head. Did she even know where she was going? His cabin was in the opposite direction. "So, will you save her from herself?"

"I don't know what to do. I need to think about it." Her agitation was obvious. She walked much faster than usual and her hands were balled into fists.

"What did she say? I knew she'd refuse you, but you seem needlessly angry."

"'Needlessly'?" She stopped abruptly and turned on him. "This entire situation is needless, but it's your fault not mine!" She shoved him hard, then started walking again.

He rocked back on his heels, but didn't lose his balance. "Tell me what she said."

"Go to hell! I've had it with all of you." She angrily wiped at her eyes and he realized she was crying. Lily never cried. Through all of the tumult, and his ongoing provocations, she'd remained cool and composed. Always in control. Her ability to think logically was one of the characteristics that appealed to him. They were both pragmatic and sensible.

Catching her upper arm, he spun her back around. "What did she say to you?" It was a demand this time.

"She didn't just refuse to reconsider, she echoed all of your arguments and reminded me that I'm—" A harsh sob interrupted her words and tears welled in her eyes.

"That you're what?" he persisted, not yet understanding her reaction.

"It doesn't matter." She tugged against his hold, lips trembling.

He kept his grip firm while being careful not to hurt her. "Clearly it does or you wouldn't be this upset."

"What difference does it make to you?" Her voice rose along with her temper. "We're not potential mates. I'm not compatible with anyone!" With a sudden burst of strength, she jerked her arm free and ran off down the corridor.

Stunned by the implication, he jogged after her. He couldn't believe what he'd just heard. Her incompatibility, *their* incompatibility was at the heart of her upset. All of her arguments and protestation led him to believe she had no interest in being claimed by anyone. Obviously, that wasn't true. Despite all her claims of indifference, she did want a mate.

He sighed as he hurried along in her wake. His life had always been solitary. He drifted from one bloody conflict to another without ever caring about the cause. He offered his skills, and his visions, to the highest bidder, knowing lives would be lost because of his insights.

Meeting Kage had restored a sense of purpose to Arton's life, but that didn't change his dismal past. He'd given up on romance a very long time ago. Lily deserved someone who could love her as deeply as she would doubtlessly love him. Arton was too jaded, too ruined, to provide what she needed in a life partner.

He was careful to keep less than ten feet between them. She'd clearly forgotten about their tether, but he'd felt the agony before and didn't care to relive the experience.

She took a lift to deck four, then headed toward the forward section of the ship. She didn't have the clearance necessary to enter restricted areas, so her destination was likely the observation platform above the command center. As he'd surmised, she climbed the ladder leading to the floor entrance. She didn't invite him to follow, yet she left the door open.

Sunlight warmed his skin as he climbed through the opening. He closed the door before he joined her at the railing. The platform was simply that, a railed area that allowed occupants to enjoy their surroundings. A transparent dome capped the circular space while the ship was in motion. Today the dome had been retracted, offering temperate breezes and fresh air. They stood side-by-side for a moment, staring out at the surrounding forest. The trees swayed hypnotically as the wind gently stirred their branches.

He wanted to touch her, pull her into his arms and comfort her, but he knew she'd only push him away. And he didn't understand the impulse. If they weren't genetically compatible, why couldn't he stop thinking about her, longing for her?

Maybe if he understood her attitude, it would help him unravel his. He chose his words carefully, needing information, not more emotional reactions. "I didn't think you were interested in a long-term relationship. What changed your mind?"

"Time and logic." She took a deep breath and rested her hands on the railing. "I was snatched from Earth thirty-four days ago. That doesn't sound like a lot of time. Many prisoners of war go for years without giving up hope of escape or rescue." She glanced at him, her features gradually relaxing as she expressed her inner turmoil. "This situation is very different. We all know there will be no rescue. Humans are incapable of long-range space travel and the battle born are overwhelmed with their own problems. Like it or not, this planet is our home now. The only thing we can control is our reaction to this inevitable situation."

She looked at him, clearly waiting for some sort of response. "Makes sense." She'd barely begun her explanation, so he wasn't sure what else to say.

"Almost all the captives volunteered for the battle born transformation program, so they were already intrigued by the idea of bonding with a Rodyte male."

Arton had used the information in the battle born database to identify potential mates for the Outcasts. It was the quickest and most accurate way of locating genetically compatible females. Besides, knowing each Outcast bride would be stolen away from an arrogant battle born soldier added to the sweetness of the adventure.

"Thea and I are exceptions, so it took us longer even to consider what you guys are offering."

"But you have considered it?" He studied her profile. She seemed more comfortable with her gaze averted.

"We've had thirty-four days with little to do but think and we're surrounded by females who keep pointing out the benefits of being bonded with a Rodyte. Health, longevity, protection, passion, family, and maybe even magic. Who wouldn't be tempted by all of that? Especially when the alternative is endless years of loneliness and resentment?" The wind caught a lock of her long dark hair and whipped it across her face. She gathered the strands with her fingertips and tucked them behind her ear. "It's also hard to be excited about life unless you have a purpose. You guys came here with very specific ideas. The women can be part of what you're trying to build, or they can wallow in self-pity for the rest of their lives." She glanced at him as she added, "That's not a very hard choice."

He only nodded, not wanting to interrupt her until she was finished.

"Thea isn't swayed by any of it, of course. She's still grieving and angry. Nothing will convince her to cooperate."

"And you? Have you been swayed by their arguments?"

She shrugged, the gesture not quite believable. "As Jillian was quick to point out, I'm no one's potential mate. The arguments don't apply to me."

Her obvious disappointment tore at his heart, stirring feelings he barely recognized in himself. "A couple doesn't have to be genetically compatible to—"

"I was fighting for my fellow captives, protecting them from their ruthless captors." She abruptly switched topics, hiding behind the less personal elements of the conflict. "According to Jillian, they're all switching sides. Now I'm an obstacle keeping them from what they want. They no longer see my refusal as noble or even helpful."

Unable to resist the impulse any longer, he lightly touched her shoulder. Awareness tingled up his arm, urging him on to more intimate touches. "You can still help them, protect them. Your role will just be different than before."

"My role would be exactly what you intended from the start." She shook her head but allowed his touch. "If I reward your bad behavior, it encourages others to misbehave. If one of the females refuses her potential mate, he might not take no for an answer. Why should he? You didn't."

He had to progress carefully. She was closer to surrender than ever before. The ruthless thought made him want to laugh. His need to touch her had nothing to do with gaining her cooperation. He desperately wanted to run his hands all over her body and hear her moan his name. "Your primary argument has been that we're forcing our will on you." He paused, watching her reaction to his statement. Her gaze narrowed a fraction, but she said nothing. "Did Jillian at least convince you that she's not being forced?"

She turned her head and gazed back out at the horizon, shifting just enough to dislodge his hand. "I'm not sure I agree. The pull is a form of coercion."

He'd heard this argument before and didn't understand the thinking. "The pull is a spontaneous biological function. Hunger urges you to eat. Do you consider that coercion?"

"How well do you know Stront?"

The abrupt subject change surprised him. She still had her face averted, so he wasn't sure what inspired the question. "He's been with us for little over a year. He does what he's told without argument and doesn't cause trouble. He's quick witted and good in a battle."

Her gaze darted toward him and then away. "That's not what I meant. Is he loyal? Can he be gentle? Will he take good care of Jillian?" Resting her hand on the railing, she looked at him but stayed just out of reach. "She's really naive. I don't want her hurt by anyone."

It was the perfect opportunity to remind her that Jillian might well be hurt unless she fixed the formula, but angering her at this point would be foolish. "Stront is both loyal and trustworthy. He's also in love with Jillian."

"She thinks she loves him too, but she's so young. I don't think she's ever been in a serious relationship."

"Soul bonding is permanent," he reminded her. "It doesn't get any more serious than that."

"You're not making me feel better." She heaved a dramatic sigh.

He fought back a smile. There were all sorts of things he could do to make her feel better, but it was seriously doubtful she'd allow any of them. "Stront is a good man. You don't need to worry about him hurting your friend."

A faint disturbance snapped Arton to high alert. He spun around, arms out to the side.

"Relax," Kage said with a lazy smile. "I come in peace." The wind caught the ridiculous cape that was part of Kage's barbarian costume. The blood-red material rippled in the wind, then wrapped around his torso, making him look like the cross between a Bilarrian brigand and a Roman Centurion. The munitions bands were loaded now. Kage never left his cabin without a variety of weapons at his disposal.

"How did you get up here?" Lily asked, her voice tremulous. "You didn't come through the door." She pointed to the floor opening, which was squarely in her line of sight.

Unlike many of his men, Kage could teleport. Most assumed that his "powers" were the result of highly sophisticated technology. He had once trained as a techno-mage after all, and passing off technology as magic was what they did best. Only Arton knew the truth. The overlord loved gadgets, especially when they mimicked paranormal gifts. However, he had genuine abilities too.

Kage ignored Lily's question, looking at Arton instead. "I know you took her to see her friends. What was the outcome?"

"Jillian refused to reconsider, but Lily's decision has yet to be determined." All the cabins were under surveillance. Kage could have found out what transpired without leaving his quarters. What did he really want?

Lily tensed as Kage turned toward her.

"The transformation program launches tomorrow. Are you willing to— Will you please ensure that no one is harmed by the process?"

Lily stared up at the overlord, shocked by his civility. She opened her mouth, but a sharp cry echoed through the trees interrupting whatever she'd been about to say.

Kage rushed to the railing and stared out across the forest. "Report!"

Arton couldn't hear the responses, but he knew Kage had opened a link with the patrol groups scattered about the forest.

"Understood. Contain it, but don't fire unless it leaves you no other choice." Without explaining what was happening, Kage teleported off the platform.

"What's going on?" Lily moved up beside him, concern and curiosity widening her gaze.

"I'm not sure." Gradually opening his mind, Arton began to scan.

"Who was Kage talking to?" Her voice became hushed, uncertain.

Arton held up one hand, backing her off without pulling his focus. It was unlikely his talents would be of any use if the guards were dealing with an "it" not a who. Besides, there was no way he was dragging Lily into danger and the tether bands made it impossible to leave her behind. She stood beside him, quiet and still, so he reached over and took her hand.

Lily's mind was chaotic, not surprising for a person with no training. He eased inward, penetrating as slowly as he could.

"What are you...oh." She gasped softly, then fell silent again.

Once his mind was linked with Lily's, he projected his being back into the woods. He glided along, spreading his energy on the wind as he absorbed images, sounds, and impressions. Surges of fear and desperation guided him toward the scene. Three guards had a creature trapped in the corner created by a rock formation and a tight cluster of trees. The animal snarled and snapped, lips pulled back from sharp-looking teeth. Its eyes flashed yellow in the dimness, but the dense shadows concealed the details of its appearance. A woman stood cowering in the embrace of an Outcast. His face was turned away, so Arton couldn't identify the burly male.

"What is that thing?" Lily whispered.

"Carnivorous predator. Indigenous. Our patrols have come across them before."

Kage approached the creature slowly, hands extended, palms out.

"What's he doing?" Concern sharpened Lily's voice.

Arton glanced at her without ending the scan. Her face was always lovely, but the soft twilight accented her high cheekbones and supple skin. She'd closed her eyes as she focused inward. His hand was halfway to her face before he realized what he was doing and lowered his arm. He had to stop touching her, no matter how badly he wanted her. She'd been interested enough to look for him in the matching database. He shouldn't give her false hope. He wasn't interested in a mate and she deserved more than what he could give her.

His hold on the forest scene began to slip, so he quickly fed energy into the scan. Kage bent to one knee, his hands still extended. The creature growled.

"Oh please, just kill it," the female murmured, her voice muffled against her male's chest.

Suddenly, the creature leapt at Kage, jaws clearly aimed at his throat. A stream of energy arced through the gloom and incinerated the creature half an instant before its claws imbedded themselves in the overlord's shoulders.

"Damn it, Torrin," Kage grumbled as he pushed back to his feet. "I told you not to shoot."

"He was going for your throat, sir." Torrin squared his shoulders and raised his chin, looking even meaner than usual. "I wasn't willing to risk it."

"That was my decision not yours," Kage insisted.

"If you say so, sir." Torrin generally followed orders, but he definitely had a mind of his own.

Lily's sharply indrawn breath drew Arton's attention away from the scene and back to her.

"What's his name?" Her voice was tense now, almost harsh. "That's the bastard who snatched me from the *Triumphant*."

"His name is Torrin, but you shouldn't blame him. *I* chose you for this project."

She snatched her hand back and opened her eyes. "You don't need to sound so proud about it."

Kage flashed back into view, saving Arton from a response. "That's the third one we've seen in the past two days. They're definitely on the offensive."

"They're defending their territory," Arton pointed out. "We can't really blame them for that."

Kage tossed back his cape and shifted his weight from foot to foot, clearly still hyped up from his interaction with the beast. "Which is why I was trying to touch its mind. We need to determine its level of intelligence."

That would have been helpful, but not at the cost of Kage's life. "Torrin was protecting you. You can't punish him for that."

"We need to know more about them. There are all sorts of prey animals in this sector, but they're the only predators we've encountered." He rolled his shoulders, and then stretched out his back. "Anyway. Back to our earlier conversation." He looked at Lily as he asked, "Are you willing to help us or not?"

Chapter Three

*A*re you willing to help us or not?

The overlord's question echoed through Lily's mind like the ominous rumble of thunder. If it were just the Outcasts pressuring her, she was prepared to resist them forever. But how could she turn her back on the very women she was trying to protect? Jillian thought she was in love with Stront. Who knew, maybe she was. And if Jillian's claim about the other captives was true, withholding the formula now would do more harm than good.

"You win." Her surrender sounded resentful and sad, an accurate representation of her mood. "I can't fight you and my fellow captives. If they honestly want this, I'll give you the formula. But I need to know for certain that bonding with your men is what the majority of them want."

"And how will you achieve this certainty?" Kage crossed his arms over his chest, accenting the defined muscles cording his entire torso. The man was enormous yet still managed to move with inherent grace.

Were Rodytes naturally leaner than humans, or did their harsh lifestyle shape their bodies? She'd started exploring the genetic differences between Rodytes and humans on the *Triumphant*, but her supervisor kept her so busy she hadn't had a lot of time for her own research. She shook away the distracting thought and explained, "Each ship housing females was asked to choose a section leader."

"I'm aware."

"I'd like each section leader to take a vote and report their findings to me."

"Done." He dipped his head, sending a lock of dark hair sliding across his forehead, momentarily obscuring one of his eyes. "Dr. Foran will meet you in main medical. He'll ensure you have everything you need."

"I need one more thing from you before I agree."

"You already agreed." His tone was more growl than grumble.

Her pulse began to race as she pushed her luck, but this was too important to ignore. "I want Thea returned to our cabin. She doesn't need another reason to hate you."

"Impossible."

She tensed, annoyed by his imperious tone. "Why is that impossible? I thought the overlord was the ultimate authority."

Her attempt to provoke him only made him chuckle under his breath. "I can't send Thea anywhere at the moment. She's no longer on this planet."

"What?" Shocked by the revelation, Lily looked from Kage to Arton and back. "Where is she?"

"I'm not sure," Kage admitted. "By the time the guards arrived to escort her to detention, Rex Dravon had taken off and Thea was gone. Scans confirmed that she's not here, so I can only conclude that Rex decided to keep her."

Lily gasped. "He can't just decide to keep her. Doesn't he work for you?"

"Depends on the day." He tossed back his cape, clearly unconcerned with the development. "Some days he works *for* me, other days he works *with* me. As long as he brings me what I need, he can word it anyway he likes."

"And you don't have a problem with him stealing one of your women?" Shock gave way to simmering anger and she slowly clenched her fists.

Kage just shrugged and she wanted to punch him, but his next revelation took the wind out of her sails. "They're potential mates. Rex is courting her. This will piss off her other five matches, but I admire his ingenuity."

"Unbelievable." She shook her head, unsure if she should be angry with or feel sorry for Rex Dravon. "He has no idea what he's done. Thea will make him so sorry he barged to the front of the line."

"Is there anything else I can do for you?" She didn't miss the subtle mockery in the overlord's voice.

She held up her arm. "Can we dispense with these? I'm sure Arton has better things to do than babysit me."

Kage looked at Arton, his expression suddenly unreadable. After a tense pause, he shook his head. "The tether bands stay until the first *successful* transformation is complete."

"That's so unfair," she cried. "Even on the *Triumphant* we weren't guaranteed success. There are too many variables."

Kage waved away her protests. "Then you better do everything in your power to compensate for them."

"You don't trust Lentar to supervise her?" Arton clenched his jaw and narrowed his eyes while his silver phitons gleamed dangerously.

"It's not Dr. Foran's job to supervise her. It's yours. End of story."

"Yes, sir." He put just enough sarcasm on the title to communicate his displeasure while not incurring the overlord's wrath.

Kage turned back to Lily. "With access to our technology and the assistance of Dr. Foran, can you have the formula ready by morning?"

She was still reeling from the overlord's casual revelations. Thea was somewhere in space with that...pirate, and Lily would be tethered to Arton until the first couple was transformed successfully. She wasn't sure what she'd done to piss off the powers that be, but it sure felt like she was under attack from some malevolent being.

"Well?" The autocratic snap in his voice revealed his impatience. Apparently, the overlord was ready to move on to the next crisis demanding his attention.

"It shouldn't be a problem." The Rodytes were closer to success than they realized. She hadn't lied when she told Arton there were errors. However, each error was negligible, only requiring a minor adjustment to the existing formula.

"It's nice to have you onboard." The overlord flashed an unexpected smile as he added, "Finally." Then he inclined his head and teleported off the observation platform.

Kage's apparent animosity toward Arton had puzzled her from the start. She'd heard they were best friends. "I understand why he's annoyed with me. What did you do to anger him?"

Arton moved closer, his gaze warm yet assessing. "Kage isn't angry with me."

"Then why did he saddle you with me. This is clearly punitive." She held up her arm again, indicating the tether band.

"Unlike most humans, Outcasts believe in accountability. I selected you to assist us, so your refusal reflected poorly on my decision."

"But I'm cooperating now. This feels vindictive."

His phitons gleamed as he moved even closer. "My DNA has been extensively altered. This makes compatibility with any female unlikely." He gripped the railing with one hand and slipped the other in his pocket as if he didn't trust himself not to touch her. "The overlord isn't punishing me. He's playing matchmaker."

"I see." She held her ground, tired of feeling vulnerable around him.

Suddenly he wrapped his hand around the back of her neck and tilted her chin up with his thumb. His smoke-colored gaze drilled into hers, demanding honesty and...surrender? "I thought his efforts were wasted until you reacted to Jillian's taunting. Are you interested in finding a mate or not?"

Was she? Not that long ago, the answer would have been a resounding no. She'd thought she was in love, even agreed to help the battle born so she could be near the object of her affection. He was a dashing Rodyte spy named Jakkin. But short weeks after Lily's arrival, Jakkin located his mate and promptly claimed her, leaving Lily alone and devastated.

She'd all but given up on romance of any kind. And then she met Arton.

"I might be." The admission sent tingles down her spine. "Under the right circumstances."

His other hand joined the first, anchoring her face at just the right angle. "Am I part of those 'circumstances'?"

"Maybe." It was an invitation and he didn't disappoint. His lips brushed against hers, then settled into place, warm and intimate. She slowly parted her lips, craving his taste. Again, he didn't hesitate. The tip of his tongue caressed her lips, rewarding her surrender. Then his arms wrapped around her, drawing her snugly against his body. She groaned at the penetrating heat and the strength so apparent in his embrace. This was what she wanted, what she dreamed of each night, as she tossed and turned in her lonely bed.

He drew back slowly, phitons glowing. "I'm not your mate, Lily. I can't give you forever. But we can share pleasure in the here and now."

He kissed her again, a deeper, hungrier exchange. She clung to him, allowing herself to exist in the moment rather than brood over all the obstacles in their way. When he pulled back the second time they were both breathless and more than ready for more.

"This has to wait." He kissed the tip of her nose and eased away from her. "Dr. Foran is waiting for you."

Actually, the entire settlement was waiting for her. The Outcasts were here to found a civilization shaped by their unconventional rules and freedom-loving philosophies. Families would be at the center of that civilization, which meant as many Outcasts as possible needed to claim their mates. She'd watched it all taking shape, knowing she would always be an outsider, among, but not one of the bonded couples.

Arton couldn't change that, but he offered an alternative. They could spend time together, enjoy "sharing pleasure", maybe even develop a genuine affection for each other. It wasn't a fairytale ending, but wasn't it better than being alone?

Lily's mind continued to race as Arton led her to main medical. There had been a connection between them from the start, a visceral awareness that drew them together. Being at cross-purposes kept them focused on their arguments, so each ignored the undeniable attraction. Now that the conflict was resolved, all she could think about was him.

She wanted to know about his life before she met him. Why didn't he speak with his brothers? She didn't know the Lux brothers well, but they seemed honorable and well-respected. Their father was still alive. When was the last time Arton spoke with him? Was his step-mother part of the conflict?

But first things first. She needed to fix the formula, which would maximize the chances of Jillian and Stront undergoing the transformation without any sort of damage.

Main medical was a large circular room with treatment stations lining the outer wall. In the center were access terminals and highly advanced 3-D printers capable of producing supplies and medications. An adjacent room contained four regeneration beds, which made traditional surgery all but obsolete. She was familiar with the arrangement. The largest clinic aboard the *Intrepid* had utilized a similar design. The hospital ship was where Lily had worked before being transferred to the *Triumphant*.

A tall, brown-haired male hurried toward them as they stepped into the room. He held out his hand toward Lily, which surprised her. Most Rodytes didn't shake hands. "I'm Lentar Foran. I'm thrilled to meet you." Deep dimples framed his mouth when he smiled and his eyes were a unique mixture of green, gold, and brown. Was he Rodyte? She'd never seen one without phitons.

"I'm pleased to meet you as well." She shook his hand.

He handed her a datapad with a video file on screen ready to be played. "Overlord Razel said you would want to see that before we begin."

"That was fast," she muttered under her breath, easily guessing what she was about to see. She activated the video and watched as all twelve section leaders reported the results of the vote one by one. As Jillian predicted, the majority of human females wanted Lily to cooperate with the Rodytes. The vote wasn't unanimous, however. About thirty-five percent were still unwilling to accept what the Outcasts had in mind for them, but the other sixty-five percent wanted the option to go through with the transformation.

"Thank you," she said after the last leader revealed her findings. Lily handed the datapad back to Dr. Foran.

"The laboratory is through there." He motioned toward an adjoining door directly across from the regen units, then set the datapad aside. "I'd like to get right to work if you don't mind. I'll need to run a serious of simulations once you've modified the formula."

"Of course." There were hundreds of details that needed to be addressed before the first attempt at transformation began. She wanted to see if he was prepared. "Do you have regen units preprogramed with Jillian's and Stront's genetic profiles?" Her team had lost a volunteer while one of the doctors frantically entered her information. It had only taken him a few minutes, but they were minutes the volunteer couldn't spare.

"I've studied Dr. Mintell's notes extensively and emulated each step he took."

She stopped walking and turned toward him. "How did you study Mintell's notes? I thought they were unable to crack the encryption on his datapad."

Arton pressed his hand against the small of her back, the gesture undeniably possessive. Did he feel threatened by the doctor? Lily hadn't really thought about it, but she supposed he was handsome. "There's more than one way to attain information," Arton said. "We received a transmission from one of our spies nine days ago. It contained pages and pages of Mintell's notes, but no formula."

"I see." She started walking again, taking herself away from his hand. It was much too early in their relationship for displays of possession.

Their relationship? A couple of kisses and they were in a relationship? Hadn't she learned anything from the fiasco with Jakkin? The surest way to get her heart broken—again—was to read more into the situation than was actually there. Arton wanted to have sex with her. That was all he'd offered.

The laboratory was small, but well organized. Lily showed Dr. Foran the two places where his formula needed to be adjusted. He made the adjustments, then sent the revised formula to one of the 3D printers. Soon they had a dozen injectors filled with the stabilizing agent.

She felt Arton's gaze on her the entire time. He sat on a stool near the door and remained silent and watchful. She sat beside Dr. Foran, their chairs huddled together so they could see the same display. Dr. Foran chatted away, his manner friendly and open. She'd clashed with her first Rodyte supervisor and the second had been introverted and secretive, so Dr. Foran's friendliness was a welcome change.

"Do you mind if I ask a personal question?" she asked as they waited for a computer simulation to reach its conclusion.

He swiveled toward her, his knee brushing against her leg. "Not at all. Ask me anything." He flashed an encouraging smile that deepened his dimples and made his hazel eyes shine.

"You don't have phitons. Is Rodymia your homeworld?"

His smile faltered. "I'm not sure I have a 'homeworld.'"

"I'm sorry. I didn't mean to pry."

Despite her willingness to let the subject drop, he took a deep breath and explained, "My mother was human. I have her eyes." He ran his hands down his thighs, smoothing out nonexistent wrinkles. The backs of his fingers brushed against her leg in the process, so Lily rotated her seat just enough to take her body out of reach. His touches were casual, almost unconscious, but they still made her uneasy. "My father was from a planet called Mejikon. I've never been there and barely remember him, so I consider myself human."

"Have you ever been to Earth?"

"No, which is the reason for my original hesitation."

Other questions swam through her mind, tempting her to venture deeper, to encourage him to share. But he was obviously uncomfortable with the topic, so she merely nodded. Thea wouldn't have hesitated. She would have pestered him with questions until she couldn't think of anything else to ask. But then, Thea's boldness was born of pain not true confidence.

The simulation concluded without complications, so Dr. Foran changed the parameters slightly and triggered another one. "You're quiet all of a sudden. What are you thinking about?"

"Thea, one of my roommates. She's gotten herself into some trouble and I'm worried about her."

The doctor reached over and patted her hand. "I'm sure she'll be fine. Humans are resilient."

Again his touch had been light and casual, but she glanced at Arton. Not surprisingly, his gaze was narrowed and his lips pressed into a disapproving line. She ignored his possessive behavior, not wanting to start a fight in front of the doctor.

They fell into a companionable silence as Dr. Foran programed simulation after simulation. Like a moth mesmerized by a flame, Lily kept looking at Arton. His expression changed each time their gazes locked. He acknowledged the contact, but said nothing.

An hour passed, and then another as they focused on the task at hand. Lily tried to fight back a yawn and failed.

The doctor smiled at her. "You don't need to stay for all of these. The computer does all the work. Besides, most of them are redundant at this point. I just believe in being thorough."

Lily hesitated, but Arton happily accepted the out. He stood and motioned her toward the door. "You haven't eaten in several hours. It's time to go."

Her first instinct was to rebel, to remain just to spite him. The tether band forced him to stay as long as she did, and that gave her a perverse pleasure.

"It's fine," Dr. Foran encouraged. "Go have something to eat. In fact, the rest of this is routine. I'll contact you if there are any surprises."

She couldn't help feeling as if she were shirking her responsibilities. Still, she'd been ordered to assist Dr. Foran, not run the entire program. Seeing no other alternative, she pushed back from the workstation and stood. "I'll see you in the morning."

"Bright and early," he warned with a goodhearted wink. "The overlord is anxious for us to get started."

Arton's mood darkened as he ushered Lily out of the clinic and back toward his cabin. Sitting idly by while she flirted with Lentar Foran had been torture. Arton had nothing against Lentar personally. He actually liked the doctor. He just didn't want any other male near her. Each time Foran touched her, it was all Arton could do to keep from flying across the room and pummeling the doctor within an inch of his life. Her scent lingered in Arton's nose, making him restless and aggressive. He needed to mark her, spread his scent all over her body so other males would know she belonged to him.

The possessive thought shocked and confused him. His being was so dark and twisted, thanks to Harbinger Guild, that Arton swore he would never inflict his moods on a female. He'd shared pleasure with a few, but a long-term relationship had seemed unattainable.

So why had he kissed Lily? If he took her to his bed without a formal commitment, it sent the wrong message to the other unmatched males. But what commitment could he offer her while still being honest? He wasn't opposed to a long-term relationship. He'd just never found a female who would put up with his dark moods for more than a few weeks. It was unlikely Lily would be any different.

He shouldn't have started this. She deserved so much more than he was able to give. But she was like an addiction. Every time he saw her, he had to be near her, and being near her made him want to touch her. And touching her only made him desperate for more, more of her taste and softness.

"I'd rather eat in one of the dining halls," she told him as they stepped off the lift and onto deck four.

She'd stopped walking, so he had no choice but to do the same. "You weren't afraid to be alone with me earlier."

"And I'm not afraid of you now," she insisted. "I just don't want to be cooped up inside a cabin, yours or mine."

He didn't believe her for a second. She was afraid he'd kiss her again, afraid they'd end up in bed. Wise woman. After watching her flirt with Lentar Foran, that was exactly what Arton wanted. He needed her spread out beneath him, arching into each thrust as he buried himself inside her.

They walked toward the officers dining hall in tense silence. She kept her hands pressed against her sides, ensuring that they didn't touch even inadvertently. "I don't want to be your mistress," she blurted suddenly. "I don't expect a fairytale ending, but I need more than recreational sex."

"'Recreational sex?'" He'd never heard the phrase before, but its meaning was obvious. "I'm offering more than that, and I think you know it."

"'We can share pleasure in the here and now,'" she quoted. "Sounds like recreational sex to me."

He clasped his hands behind his back in an effort to keep from shoving her up against the corridor wall. "I will protect you and care for you. I will—"

"Do you care for me? A few hours ago you didn't seem to like me."

They reached the dining hall and a smile tugged at the corners of his mouth. If she was determined not to be alone with him, she was out of luck. The room was empty. Not too surprising. It was eight forty-seven p.m. and females were required to be in their cabins by nine. "You can be exasperating, but I've always been interested in you."

She shot him an annoyed look. "How flattering."

The officers dining hall was small compared to the ones located on the lower levels. Six round tables each seated eight, and nutrition generators and recycle units lined the far wall. The wall to their left was currently transparent, allowing the occupants to see the surrounding forest. The surface could also be used as a display for animations or videos.

Before he could reply, she hurried across the room and activated one of the nutri-gen kiosks, quickly making her selections. Half a turkey sandwich and a glass of *blish*, the spicy citrus beverage so many of the females favored. No wonder she was so small. She ate like a bird.

"Would you rather I flatter you?" he asked. "I thought you would appreciate honesty."

She took her tray from the kiosk and headed for a nearby table. "So we have sex until the newness wears off. What then?"

Far more interested in their conversation than food, he joined her at the table. "First of all, it could take a very long time for the newness to wear off. I find sharing pleasure...well, pleasurable. Don't you?"

She ignored his question and stared into his eyes. "There's more to life than sex. And you didn't answer my question. What happens to me once you move on?"

"How would I move on? All of the other females have genetic matches. I would be depriving someone of their mate if I formed a social alliance with any of the other females." He reached over and caught her hand. "I'm sorry I can't offer you more, but neither can anyone else."

A long, ragged sigh escaped her as she pulled her hand out of his. She picked up her sandwich and muttered, "Does your honesty have to be so brutal?"

He pressed back into his chair as she began to eat. "I don't play games. That's part of the reason we ended up with these." He raised his arm, indicating the tether band. "If I'd been more willing to manipulate your emotions, it's likely we would have come to an agreement before Kage lost his temper."

She paused for a sip of *blish*. "Aren't you hungry?"

He was famished, just not for food. "Rodytes don't require food as often as humans." It was true, but it wasn't the reason he wasn't eating. Courting her, as clumsily as his effort was, had his stomach tied in knots. "It's not in my best interest to tell you this, but I really do hate the games people play with each other."

"You already told me you hate games. How is that not in your best interest?"

"That's not what I meant." And he was pretty sure she knew it.

"So tell me." She took another bite of her sandwich as she waited for his response.

"You are my only option, unless I'm willing to steal someone's mate. However, I'm not your only option."

"Really?" She'd finished her meager meal, so she wiped her mouth with a napkin. "Why is that?'

She sounded curious not hopeful, but he was already regretting his impulse toward full disclosure. "Some of the Outcasts are not battle born, and some of the battle born have chosen not to participate in the transformation program. There are nineteen males without a potential mate."

"I wondered about that, but there is nothing in the database about it." She looked beyond him as she finished her *blish*. "We ran into a couple of similar cases on the *Triumphant*. Both turned violent. Have you and the overlord anticipated the conflicts this will cause?"

"There's not much we can do proactively. We'll have to deal with each situation as it arises."

She pushed back from the table far enough so she could cross her legs. "It's not widespread on Earth, but there are those who become involved with more than one person at the same time. I think it's more common with multiple women and one man, but the reverse is not unheard of."

He shook his head, finding the suggestion amusing. "Rodytes don't share their females. We're much too possessive."

"I see." She lowered her chin and shadowed her gaze with her lashes. "Is that why you looked like you wanted to kill Dr. Foran the entire time we were working together?"

Was she flirting with him now? Desire surged through his body, momentarily stealing his breath. "You know I want you, Lily. I've made no secret of my attraction."

"You want to share pleasure with me." She didn't sound happy about the conclusion.

"I want to spend time with you, to get to know more about you and allow you to become better acquainted with me." Her hostility confused him. "Isn't this how couples interact on Earth?"

"Your right. I'm being unfair." Her words reassured, but disappointment still clouded her eyes.

"I know what you want to hear, what will ease your fears. But I will never lie to you, never make promises I have no intention of keeping. I'm offering companionship and pleasure. Anything else would be misleading."

"I appreciate your honesty, but I still think I need more."

He inclined his head, annoyed, yet understanding her disappointment. Part of him was disappointed too.

After a tense pause, she amended, "I might reevaluate my decision if you're serious about letting me know more about you."

He sighed. Why did it always come to this? Females sensed the darkness in him and wanted to understand it, they wanted to *fix* it. "What would you like to know?" The question came out like an impatient growl.

"I worked aboard the *Intrepid* and the *Triumphant*, so I met two of your brothers. Is it just you three or are there others?"

He stared back at her, his gaze drilling into hers. She had an advantage over the other curious females. She'd already guessed the source of his darkness. "*They* have another brother. His name is Dakkar. I no longer consider myself a Lux, so I have no connection to any of them."

"I see." And to his utter astonishment, she let the subject drop. "How long have you known the overlord?"

"Twenty-seven years." Now he was really confused. It wasn't like Lily to give up so easily.

"How did you meet?" She didn't sound nearly as interested in this topic as she'd been in his family history. Maybe she wasn't as interested as he'd first thought.

"Tell me about Jakkin and I'll tell you about Kage."

Cunning flashed through her gaze as she countered, "I'll tell you about Jakkin if you explain why you no longer consider yourself a Lux."

He fought back a pleased smile. Her indifference had been strategic. Good. Verbal sparring was only fun with a worthy opponent. "Fine, but not here. It's been a long day and I want to get comfortable."

"Fair enough." She stood and swept her arm toward the door. "Lead on."

Chapter Four

Arton's cabin felt smaller and less impressive as Lily entered for the second time. Sexual tension crackled between them, but she wasn't quite ready to give in. She might have spent the past month in his company, but she still knew very little about him. She moved to the sofa and sat, expecting him to choose the chair facing her. Instead, he sat beside her, near but not touching her.

"You go first," she prompted.

His brow arched and his lips curved but didn't part. "How do I know you'll keep your end of the bargain?"

"I give you my word. I will tell you whatever you want to know about Jakkin and me."

He shook his head, jaw clenching stubbornly. "You ask a question, then I'll ask a question. Even exchange."

She pressed her lips together with a sigh. "I'm not sure I know enough about your situation to ask the right questions. Fine. I'll go first." The story was embarrassing and sad—mainly because it revealed how pathetic she was—but she was far enough from the events now to talk about them without breaking down. "I met Jakkin seven years ago when one of his missions on Earth went horribly wrong. He was injured and broke into my lab, hoping to find medical supplies."

Arton watched her intently, but said nothing.

"I knew I should call the cops, but he begged me not to. His appearance was disguised, so I didn't realize he was an alien. I thought he was some sort of spy or maybe special ops on some secret mission."

His brows bunched up over his nose as his gaze narrowed. "Why not a drug dealer or a well-trained criminal? Why make him brave and noble?"

"He was wearing a belt with all sorts of sophisticated gadgets, and his speech was accented yet formal. He sounded as if he'd learned English from a language professor. There was no way he was a common criminal."

"So you decided not to involve the authorities." He stretched out his arm, resting it on the back of the sofa less than an inch from her shoulders.

The move was subtly possessive and utterly transparent. Already he was growing restless, anxious to move on. Well, she wasn't finished torturing him, and torturing herself. Revisiting this story was a good reminder of why she couldn't trust her feelings regarding Rodyte males. "I took him back to my apartment and he stayed for three days."

"Were you lovers?" He found the idea upsetting if the tension in his voice was any indication.

"No. I was more than willing, but he wasn't interested."

Arton scoffed. "I don't believe that. You're gorgeous. Trust me, he was interested."

The careless compliment pleased Lily more than she cared to admit. Not being compatible with anyone was hard on the ego. "Well, whatever his motivation, he never touched me."

She hadn't meant it as an invitation, but he moved his hand from the sofa to the back of her neck. "How did he explain his departure? Where did he say he was from?"

"He didn't. I woke up one morning and he was just gone. No note, no explanation, just gone. He never even told me his name."

His fingers caressed her skin with featherlight touches, sending tingles down her spine. "Were you angry or saddened by his ruthless behavior?"

His phrasing made her smile. "I never thought of it as ruthless, but I suppose it was. He used me without a second thought and I foolishly romanticized the entire episode. He became this man of mystery, pining away for the woman he'd had no choice but to leave behind. The truth was a little less flattering."

He stopped rubbing and gently squeezed. "Meaning?"

"He didn't think about me at all until the battle born needed a geneticist. Then he used my attraction to him to recruit me for their cause."

"How long were you lovers before he found his mate?"

She laughed softly. "I hate to disappoint you, but Jakkin and I were never lovers. He made it clear that our relationship would be completely professional as soon as I agreed to help them."

"And yet his image lingers in your mind."

That got her attention. She shifted away from his hand, pivoting her entire body to face him. "How would you know what images linger in my mind? It's against Rodyte law to scan without permission."

"Outcasts don't concern themselves with Rodyte laws." He lowered his arm, his expression unapologetic. "We live by our code of conduct and no other."

"The Outcast code of conduct allows for mental invasions?" She wasn't sure why she was so upset. She'd used every tool at her disposal to spy on him. He just had tools available to him that she didn't.

"Relax. I barely penetrated your shields. Obviously, I didn't harm you."

"That doesn't excuse it. You violated my trust." She shot to her feet, wishing she could storm from the room.

"I'm sorry." He caught her wrist and tried to pull her back down beside him. She stubbornly dug in her heels. "I shouldn't have scanned you without permission. I will never do so again."

She wasn't sure she believed him. She'd had no idea he'd done it the first time, so how would she know if he kept his word? Empowered people were so frustrating.

Releasing a ragged sigh, she returned to the sofa, but put as much space between them as possible.

After a long pause, he asked, "If Jakkin didn't seduce you, what did he do?"

"The bastard charmed me all over again. I knew we weren't compatible, and he was holding out for a mate, so we'd never be more than friends. Jakkin can be very likable when he wants to be."

"Then you watched him court and claim his mate, wishing all the while that it was you." He shook his head, but she saw compassion not pity in his eyes.

"And don't forget that's not where the story ends." His brows drew together. She'd clearly confused him. "I was kidnapped a second time and forced into a situation even more humiliating than the first. On this world I'm the *only* female not genetically compatible with one or more of the males. At least on Earth there were lots of others unworthy of being a mate."

He took her hand, intertwining their fingers. "If you're 'unworthy', so am I."

She tried to smile and failed. "I appreciate the sentiment, but that doesn't change the fact that I will never have children of my own now."

For a long silent moment, he just stared at her. "Is that important to you?"

She'd always wanted children, but she hadn't made it a priority in her life. She focused on school, then establishing her career, and then one crucial research project after another. "It was more like an item on my bucket list than something I was actively pursuing." He smiled, so she didn't explain the reference. "Well, that's my shameful secret. Now tell me yours."

He let go of her hand and pressed back into the cushions. "Which one. I have so many."

He ended the statement with a smile, but she sensed the tension behind his words. No one joined a group of outlaws without burning a few bridges along the way. "Why do you call yourself Heretic?" Maybe if she started with the obvious, she could ease into the darker parts of his past.

"I didn't choose the title." He already sounded defensive. This wasn't good. "I was *branded* a heretic when I refused to accept the nonsense they were preaching at Harbinger Academy."

Unadulterated hatred flared in his eyes as he said the word branded. Dread dropped into her stomach like a stone. "Do you mean that literally?" Her throat was so tight she barely got the question out.

He stood and tugged his T-shirt out from inside his jeans, then peeled the garment off over his head. Well-defined muscles rippled with each movement, momentarily distracting her from the images displayed on his smooth skin. Horrified, yet mesmerized, she pushed to her feet and lightly ran her fingers over the deep scar centered above his heart. A Rodyte word had been burned into his flesh in stylized letters. The scar was raised and discolored yet perfectly legible. She shuddered, unable to imagine the pain he must have endured.

"This means heretic?" She knew the answer, but needed to hear him confirm it.

"Yes." He said nothing more.

"How could they... I'm so sorry."

He grabbed her wrist and jerked her hand away. "I don't want your pity."

"I don't pity you. You've clearly used the pain they inflicted to make you strong. You took the word they meant to shame you and wear it like a badge of honor."

His fingers relaxed around her wrist, but didn't let go. "If rejecting the lies they teach makes me a heretic, I accept the title gladly."

"Someone mentioned a change in the leadership of Harbinger Guild. Are things any better now?"

He shrugged. "I've had no contact with anyone associated with Harbinger Guild since I left the academy."

She moved closer, resting her free hand on his chest. "But you didn't just leave. You were rescued by the people you claim to hate." His free arm wrapped around her waist, pulling her flush with his body. He still held her wrist slightly out to the side. The position made her smile. "Shall we dance?"

"I have a better idea." He released her wrist and lightly fisted the back of her hair. His head lowered slowly, giving her plenty of time to turn away.

She didn't. She wanted to kiss him, wanted to feel the tingling rush that accompanied his other kisses. He excited her, fascinated her, and she was tired of pretending otherwise. Her lips were slightly parted when his mouth settled over hers.

He made a soft, throaty sound as he accepted the invitation. His tongue teased her lips for a moment then pushed deeper, exploring the interior of her mouth. She rubbed her tongue against his, greeted him with open enthusiasm.

Her fingers splayed against his side, but his naked torso was too much of a temptation. She ran her hands over his arms and back, savoring the heat and muscular contours she'd been imagining for weeks. He was glorious, lean and overtly male. She wanted him, wanted passion to burn away reality. And he obviously wanted her. Ever since the battle born arrived on Earth she'd been focused on the greater good rather than her personal happiness. Well, she was ready to be selfish, if only for a while.

They continued to kiss as Arton opened the front seam in her uniform top. The Outcasts had managed to scale their garments for the much smaller bodies of their females, but they didn't have a molecular pattern for undergarments. As a result, the simple motion bared Lily's breasts.

He covered one soft mound, giving her a little squeeze before moving on to its twin. His thumb circled her nipple, then lightly rasped the tip, experimenting until he found which movements made her react.

Both nipples were hard and tingly by the time he kissed his way down her neck. She arched helplessly, rubbing her belly against the hard proof of his need for her. He felt amazing and she wanted to explore him, wanted to wrap her fingers around him and take him deep into her body.

"Gods, Lily. You're so beautiful." He whispered the words as his lips found one of her nipples. His lips parted and he sucked the beaded tip into his mouth.

She moaned, the firm suction sending need spiraling through her body.

He broke away suddenly and caught her wrist. "Not here." Half leading, half dragging her behind him, he guided her into the adjoining bedroom. He let go long enough to tug off his boots and socks and unfasten his pants.

Following his lead, she kicked off her shoes and shrugged out of her shirt. Her hands trembled as she reached for the fastener at the front of her pants. Was she really going to do this? He wasn't a potential mate. This might be nothing more than a one-night stand. The possibility decreased the heat of her passion, threatening to snuff out the flame completely.

He sighed. "If you're not ready for this, I'll wait until you are. I don't want to—"

His eyes rolled back in his head and his body crumpled to the deck at her feet.

Lily let out a startled cry as she knelt at his side. He was breathing, but he was completely unresponsive. Pausing long enough to straighten out the leg twisted up under him, she snatched her top off the floor and ran for the cabin's main door. She slipped on the shirt, hurriedly reactivating the seam as she went.

Halfway across the living room the tether band engaged, sending pulses of pain all through her body. She screamed, grabbing her head as her knees buckled. Frantically scuttling backward, she managed to reverse course long enough to deactivate the tether. Pain still echoed through her body, but it receded enough to let her think. "Hello! Help!! Medical emergency!" she screamed at the top of her lungs, terrified that no one would hear her.

The outer door slid open and the overlord hustled in. He was bare to the waist as he'd been earlier, but without the cape or munitions harness the display was much more noticeable. Arton's physique was impressive, while Kage terrified.

"What's wrong?" He looked around impatiently. "Where's Arton."

"In there." She pointed toward the bedroom. "He's having some sort of seizure."

Kage rushed across the room, snatching her off the floor by the upper arm as he went. She barely got her legs beneath her fast enough to keep from being dragged behind him. His massive hand let go just as suddenly as it had closed around her arm. He knelt at Arton's side and felt for a pulse. Then the overlord spread his fingers wide, not an inch from Arton's face. Pale blue light erupted from Kage's palm, casting Arton's features into high relief. Kage slowly passed his hand over his friend, progressing slowly from head to foot.

Lily stood back and watched in awe as the overlord scanned Arton. "Is he all right?"

Kage looked up and Lily gasped. His dark gaze was now shot through with ribbons of emerald green. And even more astonishing, the colors seemed to swirl, shifting and changing like the crystals inside a kaleidoscope. "He's having a vision," he announced casually. "If he's still out in an hour, yell for me again."

And just like that the overlord strode from the room, leaving Lily fearful and confused.

The images swirled through Arton's mind, stimulating his body as well as his intellect. Long strands of opalescent hair slid over a pale white body. Graceful fingers grasped a sleekly muscled back, the pointed nails digging in hard enough to draw blood. The male's powder-blue hair was short and mussed as if the female had run her fingers through it repeatedly. She straddled his hips, riding him vigorously with an ages old rocking motion. As she tossed back her hair and cried out sharply, Arton was able to see their faces for the first time. They had angular features and wide almond-shaped eyes that shimmered like colorless crystals, slashing cheekbones and nearly pointed chins. They looked like the mythical elves so popular on Earth.

But why was he seeing them?

The female climbed off her lover and slipped on a shiny black robe. "You may go."

The male looked annoyed and disappointed, but he gathered up his clothing and obeyed.

Thick furs cushioning her feet as she strolled across the cavernous room. Two massive creatures fell into step, one on either side of the willowy female. Arton tensed and trepidation gripped his muscles, making his heart pound. They were the same sort of predators that had attacked their patrol teams, yet they responded to the female as if they were trusted pets. Roughly the size of Earth's female lions, their shape was largely feline, yet they had no fur. Instead they had thick, grayish-black skin that was armored like a reptile.

She stood before a strange device, her hands extended, palms out. Encased in rough-hewn stones, the inner segments were smooth and glowing. Did the strange stones give off heat? Was that why she reached toward them?

The animal on her left growled and its head snapped toward the door, golden eyes suddenly glowing. The armor plating on its neck stood up, forming a defensive ruff and making it look even more like a weaponized lion.

She spoke a word Arton didn't understand and the creature lay down, the ruff relaxing against its muscular neck. It propped its huge head on even bigger paws and closed its eyes, but its conical ears rotated slowly, likely scanning for audible signs of danger.

She spoke again, though Arton couldn't understand her and a different male stepped into the room. This one's hair was blue as well, but the hue was brighter, more vivid. She turned from the glowing devise and watched her visitor approach.

Must those beasts accompany you night and day? He sent the thought directly to her mind, which allowed Arton to understand him. Arton wasn't sure why, but telepathic communication seemed to have a common language, at least in his visions.

Most days I prefer karrons to you, she thought with an unapologetic smile. *My battle cats are better behaved.*

The male didn't react to her provocation. Instead he thought, *If you continue with this recklessness, someone will catch you. It's forbidden to venture above, and you know it.*

The female shrugged, clearly unconcerned. *So they catch me. And then what? The Guiding Council is filled with old men and cowards.*

I'm on the Guiding Council, he reminded with a glare.

She just smirked. *I'm aware.*

Well, I wasn't talking about the council. I was talking about them. If they catch you, you will—

They are invaders! They don't belong here.

And as abruptly as the vision came to Arton, it disengaged.

He gasped, blinking repeatedly as he waited for his eyes to clear.

"Oh, thank God. Are you all right?" Lily's worried tone helped him shake away the shadows from his mind. He didn't want to frighten her, had no idea why the vision had gripped him so suddenly. His muscles protested as he sat up and looked around. Visions always drained his energy, and this one had been particularly vivid. He was on the floor in his bedroom and she was on her knees beside him. "I'm fine, but I need to tell Kage what I saw."

Using the bed for support, he struggled to his feet. She rushed to his side and wrapped his arm around her shoulders. "You're shaking. Are you sure you're all right?"

"The weakness will pass." To prove his point, he removed his arm and headed for the door on wobbly legs.

She followed him into the living room, looking concerned and a bit afraid. His jeans sagged a bit more with each unsteady step. He realized they were unzipped and quickly righted them. "Sorry about the interruption." He smiled at her, but she still looked upset. "Why don't you stay here? I won't be long."

"I couldn't, even if I wanted to." She held up her arm, displaying the tether band. "Besides, I'd really like to hear what you saw."

"Fair enough," he muttered and stepped out into the corridor. His legs stopped shaking, but he still felt horribly drained.

"Figured you'd be by." Kage motioned him inside. The overlord was dressed in jeans and a T-shirt, making Arton feel underdressed for a change. "Have a seat," Kage said to no one in particular. "You look like shit."

Lily and Arton chose chairs while Kage sat on the sofa, arms spread out to either side.

"Why did you figure I'd be by?" Arton asked as Kage's comment registered in his sluggish brain.

Kage laughed. "Lily screamed her head off when you went down. I thought you were trying to kill her."

"I screamed my head off when the tether band engaged," she corrected. "Thanks for that, by the way."

Another chuckle rumbled through his chest. "She does have some spirit I see. Good. There's nothing worse than a cowering female."

"Do you want to hear about my vision or not?" He was honestly too tired to care.

"Always." Kage banked his amusement, but his dark eyes still gleamed.

"I saw two beings, well, three if you count the very beginning. I hesitate to call them humanoid. They were ethereal and...elfish is the only word that fits."

"Describe them in more detail."

"The female had the most extraordinary hair. Down to her knees, and it shimmered with iridescent colors like a fire opal.

And her eyes looked like crystal, colorless yet intensely reflective. Both males had blue hair and the strange crystalline eyes. All three were tall and lithe."

"And what do these colorful elves have to do with us?" The question was tinged with mockery, but Arton didn't take offense. He would have been skeptical too.

"I wasn't sure they had anything to do with us until two of the predators that have been attacking our guards appeared at her side." He gave Kage a moment to absorb the implication. "They're called karrons, by the way. I'm pretty sure that was their species, not an individual name. She called them her battle cats." Kage just stared at him, so Arton asked, "How sure are the scout teams that this planet is uninhabited?"

Kage shook his head. "The science teams ran every scan in existence before they recommended this planet. Both Scarlett and Rhett are uninhabited."

"But Rhett hasn't always been," Arton pointed out. "Several of their reports mentioned ruins."

"Yes, ruins," Kage stressed. "Crumbling cities from long dead civilizations." He straightened, rubbing his scruffy chin as he often did when he was deep in thought. Suddenly, he shook his head and said, "It must have been an echo, a psychic memory of the beings that once lived here."

Arton wasn't convinced, but he nodded. "I was able to understand part of what they said to each other, and it sure as hells sounded like they were talking about us. She called us 'invaders' and insisted that we didn't belong here."

"I awarded Torak the *Relentless*. I'll have him rerun the scans."

"The male told her it was forbidden to, how did he put it? Venture above. Do the scans penetrate the surface?"

Kage scooted to the edge of the cushions and rested his forearms on his knees. "They can, but it's time-consuming and mind-numbingly tedious."

"Give Torak my apologies, but I think it needs to be done."

"Understood. I'll tell him."

"Thank you." Arton stood and held out his hand toward Lily.

She stood as well, but slipped her hands into her pockets, her gaze darting toward Kage then away. Her expression was tense and uncertain, not intrigued, so he guided her toward the door with his hand at the small of her back.

The privacy panel slid closed behind them and she shivered. "That man scares me to death."

He smiled. "He has that effect on a lot of people." He scanned open his door and they walked inside before she responded.

"But not you. Why aren't you intimidated by him?"

"I've known him forever, long before he was overlord."

"Really?" Curiosity burned away her unease. "How did you meet?"

He sighed, frustrated by their digression. "Are we really going to do this tonight? I'm exhausted and grumpy."

"All right." She didn't sound pleased, but she let it go. He took her by the hand and led her away from the door. "Is the *Relentless* a ship?"

"Yes. It's the flagship, newest and best in our fleet. The warlords were at each other's throats until Kage reassigned it."

"Reassigned it?" Her steps lagged as they neared the doorway leading to his bedroom. She tugged her hand out of his as she asked, "Who commanded it before?"

Too tired to confront her hesitation, he just stopped and faced her. "Kage. The *Relentless* is his pride and joy. It just about killed him to give it up."

"When he moved to the *Viper*." She nodded finally understanding the sequence of events. "Why does the overlord trust this Torak to take care of his pride and joy?"

"Like the ship, Torak Payne is our best and brightest. He was the only real choice." He took her hand again and continued toward the bedroom. The tension in her arm warned him that the passionate moment was long past. "I really am exhausted. I need sleep, and so do you."

She motioned toward the sofa. "Can't we drag it closer to the bedroom?"

He stopped and framed her face with his hands. "I will never touch you in a sexual way unless you welcome the exchange. There is no reason for your fear."

She lowered her lashes as color erupted on her cheeks. "That's not what I'm worried about. I'm not sure I can keep my hands to myself. Can you put a shirt on?"

He'd forgotten he was shirtless. "Of course." It pleased him that she found him tempting, but he'd meant what he said. He wouldn't join his body with hers until there was no doubt about her willingness. He moved to the inset dresser and pulled out a clean undershirt.

"Are you considered a warlord?"

He put on the clingy white garment before answering her question. "I'm a sorcerer. Haven't you heard?" He punctuated the question with a grin.

"Warlords and elves and sorcerers." She laughed. "Sounds like I'm trapped in a video game."

"No. You're just on an alien planet far away from Earth."

Her smile faded and she walked to the bed and pulled down the covers. "I don't need the reminder. Evidence is everywhere I look."

Her feet were bare, but she climbed into bed fully dressed. "You're going to sleep in your clothes?"

"Yes, and so are you."

Knowing better than to argue with the determination in her eyes, he just smiled and climbed in beside her. She immediately rolled to her side, facing away from him. He slipped one of his arms under her neck and wrapped the other around her waist. She tensed, but didn't object.

"Lights to ten percent." He snuggled in closer and buried his face in her hair. "Rest well," he whispered.

"You too."

Despite the temptation in his arms, blissful sleep immediately claimed him.

ARTON WAS STILL A CHILD when he learned the difference between regular and prophetic dreams. Regular dreams were soft, surreal, and often nonsensical. Prophetic dreams, by comparison, were harsh and intrusive. They always left him feeling invaded and slightly abused. He hadn't asked for this gift, hadn't undergone medical procedures to attain it as so many harbingers did. His kind—those born with their powers already active—were known as organic. And their abilities were always vast, and extremely hard to control.

An oppressive weight settled over his body, paralyzing his muscles while opening his mind. He'd learned not to struggle against the feeling, resistance brought horrible pain. Reality faded until he hung suspended in a pitch-black void. No color, no motion, no sound, just an endless blackness. This part could last for hours. It was one of the reasons he tried so hard to summon visions while he was awake, rather than letting them happen spontaneously. When he was awake, his chances of controlling the progression were increased greatly.

A female's throaty moan penetrated the darkness and his heart began to pound. This was how the other vision started. Would he now learn more about his "elves"? He wanted to know more about them, needed to understand why he'd seen them in the first place. Nothing was more frustrating than a segmented vision with no context or apparent meaning.

The moaning grew louder and Arton sighed. It was not the same voice. This one was pitched higher. She sounded younger.

His body floated down through the blackness. Currents of warm air caressed his bare skin. He was naked, which didn't surprise him. People were often naked in his visions. He felt the air around him change. It seemed to crackle with electricity.

Suddenly he was hovering over a ship's cabin. A couple shared pleasure on the narrow bunk. The male was on top, as Rodytes preferred it. He could barely see the female. She clung to the male, arms and legs wrapped around him as he moved with obvious purpose between her thighs.

He didn't need to see her face to know this was Jillian and Stront. But was this confirmation of the course everyone planned to take, or some sort of warning?

As if hearing his grumbling thought, the vision shifted. Jillian, now fully dressed, wandered through dense trees. "Stront?" Fear twisted her delicate features as she called out for her mate again and again. The leaves were green not turquoise as they were on Rhett. How strange.

"Stront! This isn't funny. Where are you?" She huddled against one of the trees, looking utterly miserable. "I'm sorry I failed you," she sobbed. "What did I do wrong?" Hard sobs shook her shoulders and she buried her face in her hands.

Arton woke up with a gasp, confused and shaken. He was sitting up, though he couldn't remember moving. He looked at Lily. She lay as she'd been all night, curled up on her side. It was amazing that he hadn't disturbed her. Even so, he was glad she was resting well.

The vision was clearly a warning, but what did he really know? Jillian would fail, that much was clear. Did anything else matter? The couple could still bond naturally. Stront would eventually accept life as it was now.

Arton released a heavy sigh and lay back down. He had to tell them. If they chose to ignore the warning and progress with the transformation, there was nothing else he could do about it. With his course of action solidified, he willed himself back to sleep.

Chapter Five

Something soft yet prickly tickled Lily's cheek. She brushed it away, sleepily rolling to her back. The sensation returned, only on her lips. She murmured softly, annoyed by the disturbance. She'd been having the sweetest dream. She was stretched out on a beach, watching Arton swim. His naked body stretched and pulled, muscles rippling as he propelled himself through the clear green water.

"Wake up, love. Everyone's waiting for you."

She blinked repeatedly, loath to let go of the peaceful dream. He lay beside her, propped on one forearm, while he stroked her face with a lock of her long hair. "What time is it?"

"Five thirty, but there's a complication. I need to speak with Stront and Jillian before you guys begin."

Fully awake now, she sat up and stretched out her back. The vague ache between her thighs reminded her that their passion had been interrupted last night. Apparently, they didn't have time to finish what they'd started either, so her neglected body would have to wait.

"I don't know about you, but I need a shower," he announced as he climbed off the bed.

Shower? As in get naked and soap up one's body? She looked toward the door leading to the adjoining bathroom. It could be entered from the bedroom or the living room. And it had been surprisingly large. The room was long and narrow. There was at least ten feet between the shower stall and either of the doors.

"How is that going to work?" she asked.

He shrugged. "It's probably best if we shower separately, being that we don't have time to linger."

"I agree, but how do we make that happen with a ten-foot leash connecting us?"

His features scrunched together and he shook his head. "I'm not ashamed of my body. Are you?"

"No, but I don't make a habit of showering in front of men who..."

He stalked toward her as she spoke, a predatory gleam in his eyes. "Men who what? You know very well that we would be lovers if we hadn't been interrupted right now. I've already seen your breasts. Your body is lovely. Now, stop being such a prude." He slapped her on the ass to accent his point.

She laughed and headed for the bathroom. He was right, she was being ridiculous. This was the twenty-first century, for pity's sake. If she wanted to get naked in front of an alien, no one would care. Certainly not said alien.

She undressed and put her uniform in the recycler. This had become a daily ritual. The Outcasts refused to make underwear for them, so most of the humans printed new uniforms each morning. The shower felt wonderful. The spray was super fine, but it spurted out from all over, wetting her entire body at once.

"I had a second vision last night." The seriousness in his tone told her to pay attention.

She opened her eyes and looked at him. He'd stripped down to his jeans and sat on the closed commode, looking every bit as grim as he sounded. "Is that why you want to talk to them before we begin?"

He nodded. His gaze dipped to her breasts, then immediately returned to her face. The bottom half of the enclosure was frosted, so he couldn't see any more than he'd already seen. She'd made sure her back was to him as she got in.

"What did you see?" she prompted when he didn't offer an explanation on his own.

"I saw them forming the bond, so I suspect the warning won't matter. Still, I have to try."

"What else happened in the vision? Why do you consider it a warning?"

"Sorry. Can you turn back around? You're very distracting like this."

Pleased by his admission, she turned her back to him and activated the cleansing mist. The fresh-smelling foam was a shampoo, body wash, deodorant and moisturizer all in one.

"I saw Jillian wandering through the trees. She was clearly lost and terrified. She called out to Stront over and over."

"That's horrible, but I don't see what it has to do with the transformation."

"The leaves were green, not turquoise, so the images were symbolic not literal. She also asked what she'd done wrong and apologized for failing him."

She quickly rinsed off the mist and smoothed her hair back from her face. He handed her a large towel as she opened the shower door. She wasn't sure if she should wrap it around her body or contain her dripping hair. Seeing her quandary, he handed her a second towel.

"I've been so focused on the formula that I almost forgot about the guide."

"What guide?"

"The volunteers back on Earth started calling it the Ghost Guide. I was fascinated by the stories, but my investigation into the accounts found no evidence that it actually existed. I'm pretty sure it's a myth, a way for humans to explain sensations and experiences they don't understand."

"Well, what do the stories claim? What does this Ghost Guide do?"

"She or it, helps them figure out what needs to be done to free their mate's magic. It always appeared to the female and the process for freeing the magic was different with each male. It all sounded very...surreal."

"Why is this only coming up now?"

"I'm a scientist," she objected. "I checked out their stories and offered a rational explanation. Can I help it if they all prefer the myth?"

"So you don't think it's an actual entity? There are more incorporeal beings than corporeal beings by far. Humans are just unaware of most of them."

She hated it when he got all superior, so she just waved away the subject. "If you're sure they'll disregard the warning, should we even bring it up. I don't want to compromise Jillian's confidence. It might become a self-fulfilling prophesy."

With a casualness she hadn't quite mustered, he shed his jeans and stepped into the shower. She got one glimpse at his fabulous ass before his lower body was obscured by the frosted panels. *Damn*. She couldn't fight back a guilty smile.

"I'm morally obligated to tell them what I saw. What they do with the information is up to them. I won't interfere."

As Arton feared, his warnings had no effect on the love-sick couple. They insisted that the program continue as planned and both Lily and Dr. Foran agreed. Preliminary scans established baseline readings for their vital signs. The injections were administered, and the couple went back to Stront's cabin to indulge fully in bonding fever.

"Now only time will tell if we got it right," Dr. Foran sounded wistful, so Lily only nodded.

"HOW LONG DOES IT TAKE to know if the transformation is successful?"

Lily pulled her gaze away from the diagram she'd been analyzing and looked at the overlord. He'd just entered the lab undetected. She still didn't understand how a man that huge could move without a sound. "The first forty-eight hours are the most important, but we never declared a transformation stable for at least a week."

He looked at the segmented wall display, then back at her. "Why aren't you supervising them?" Today he was dressed in a khaki uniform just like most everyone else, but it did little to hinder the intensity of his presence.

"Jillian and Stront are in the grip of bonding fever." She blushed hotly. "We're monitoring their vital signs. If anything unexpected happens, I'll beam them to sick bay."

"'Beam them to sick bay'?" His forehead crinkled for a moment, and then he laughed. "*Star Trek*, of course. All this must feel very strange to you."

"Not as strange as it would have a few months ago. Interacting with the battle born sort of desensitized me."

His only response was a thoughtful nod. Then he turned to Arton who was sitting on a stool nearby, looking bored and restless. "Torak's preliminary scans identified a network of caverns not far from this location. There are no life signs, but he's investigating more thoroughly."

"Thanks." Arton started to say something else, but Kage just shook his head and left the lab. "Stubborn fool," Arton muttered once the overlord had gone.

She looked at Dr. Foran, but he was so engrossed in the holographic display of the couple's vital signs that he'd missed the entire exchange.

"Is there a problem?" she asked.

He finally looked at her, his expression tense. "I'm not sure. Jillian's pulse rate is borderline dangerous."

"That's not too surprising, all things considered." Jillian was doubtlessly having the most intense sex of her young life, and Lily couldn't help feeling envious. She'd been well on her way to a similar experience when Arton's vision derailed the train.

"Still, I'm going to activate surveillance. If sex makes you uncomfortable, avert your gaze."

Sex didn't make her uncomfortable. Watching other people have sex made her uncomfortable. Still, she was a scientist, and she'd supervised more transformations than anyone here. Which, in all honesty, wasn't saying that much.

Dr. Foran activated the surveillance feed in Stront's cabin. Lily gasped and looked away, but it was too late. The image was seared on her memory. Jillian was sprawled sideways across the bunk, while Stront knelt on the bunk. Her slender legs draped his shoulders and his dark head was buried between her thighs.

"You're right. She's just enjoying herself." Dr. Foran's voice was filled with laughter.

She whipped her head around and glared at him. "You did that just to embarrass me. Didn't you?"

"Who me?" He even managed to sound innocent, but his hazel eyes twinkled with mischief. Thankfully, he'd deactivated the surveillance feed, allowing the new couple some semblance of privacy.

She looked at Arton and blushed all over again. He was staring at her with such blatant hunger that it made her nipples tingle. "It will likely be hours before they come up for air," she told Dr. Foran. "I think I'll go stretch my legs."

"Take your time," Dr. Foran advised. "I'll contact you if anything changes."

Arton fell into step beside her as she reached the corridor outside main medical, not that he had much choice. The stupid tether bands were a real nuisance. Waking up in Arton's arms had been wonderful. It felt intimate and safe, peaceful. But getting ready had been awkward at best. If they were lovers, she would have just joined him in the shower, problem solved. Instead, she'd been stuck in the utility room, pretending not to peek at his amazing body. As with everything, Arton refused to pretend. He sat on the closed commode, watching her silently. She'd kept her back turned as much as possible, but she could still feel his gaze moving all over her naked form.

They were stuck in a strange sort of limbo. She'd accepted that sleeping with him was inevitable. She wanted him too badly to resist him much longer. Still, she wanted answers to a few of her questions before she gave in.

"Let's go outside," she suggested. "I don't know how you guys survive for months on end without the sun on your face. I would not make a good long-distance traveler."

"You get used to it, eventually. I once went for three and a half years without setting foot on stationary ground."

Shocked, she looked up at him. "Seriously?"

"We were in the middle of one of the bloodiest wars I every fought so the time actually passed quickly. Still, it felt good to disembark once it was over."

"How many wars have you fought in?" She knew he was a mercenary. They all were. Still, it bothered her to picture him participating in actual warfare. He seemed too mystical for such brutality.

"Dozens, maybe hundreds." He shrugged, but his indifference seemed forced. "I stopped counting a long time ago." His dispassionate mask slammed into place as effective as a no trespassing sign.

She sighed softly. His unwillingness to share was frustrating. Besides, his cryptic claim only confused her. Dozens, maybe hundreds? How could that be? Even if he'd become a mercenary in his teens, which was unlikely, he couldn't have been fighting wars for more than fifteen or twenty years. She looked at his chiseled profile and unlined skin. There was no way he was in his forties.

He's not human! Her inner voice reminded. And Rodytes lived much longer than humans. It was amazing that after all the months working with the battle born, and another month here, she could still judge him by human standards.

They took a lift to deck one, meaning to exit the ship through one of the large common areas. The cafeteria/lounges on each of the twelve ships were a popular gathering spot for the females. Heads turned as Lily walked by with Arton. His silver-and-black hair made him easy to identify. Everyone knew the overlord's "pet harbinger". She'd never had the nerve to ask him, but he likely hated the nickname. She certainly would.

"Lily," Sara called out, waving wildly. Lily waited while Sara wove her way through the crowded tables and joined them to one side of the wide center aisle. "How is Jillian? Please tell me they both survived the procedure."

"The 'procedure' is simply a series of injections. We took baseline readings of their vital signs, gave them the injections and sent them to Stront's cabin to do what nature has been urging them to do."

Sara's dark eyes narrowed and she tilted her head. "Then how do they transform into whatever they're supposed to become?" Arton tried to disguise his laugh as a cough, but Sara wasn't fooled. She turned on him, hands on hips, one of her favorite poses. "Don't you laugh at me. I might not understand how it works, but at least I haven't agreed to anything." She shook her head, thick dark hair swishing around her shoulders. "I can't believe how many of these fools want to go next, and they haven't even heard if Jillian lived or died."

"She was very much alive the last time we checked in on her." Lily glanced at Arton and they shared a knowing smile.

"Good, then answer my question. If it's not a surgical procedure, how are they transformed?"

There was plenty of information in the data base regarding transformation, but Lily had to admit that much of it was filled with medical terminology. She was a geneticist and she still struggled to understand parts of it. She was still trying to simplify the concepts in her mind when Arton moved closer to Sara.

"When a Rodyte male claims his mate he anchors what is known as a soul bond. It's a connection between their minds that allows them to share thoughts and emotions. This process also triggers changes in his body and hers."

Other women began to gather around, clearly interested in his explanation. Or were they just curious about him? Arton the Heretic was notorious.

Trying to relate it to something Sara already understood, Lily said, "Think of it as a second puberty. Their bodies receive hormones and genetic instructions that customize their bodies specifically for each other. This maximizes their chances of producing children and makes them even more appealing to each other."

"Oh boy!" one of the onlookers cried. "I'm not sure mine could be any more appealing than he is already." Laughter and whispered comments rippled through the rapidly growing crowd.

"Because their bodies are already changing," Lily went on, not wanting them to lose sight of the original question. "We use the opportunity to engineer additional changes." She started to explain that the targeted mutations created a genetic synchronization, radically decreasing the chances of rejection, then realized she was starting to sound like the database. "His DNA absorbs elements of hers and hers takes on elements of his. The changes are actually given to the female and she passes them to the male."

"That's all well and good, but how will we free their magic without the Ghost Guide?" A slender young woman with short auburn hair and semi-hostile eyes pushed her way to the front of the crowd. "My sister is on the *Triumphant* and she told me it can't be done without a guide."

Lily tensed. She'd fervently hoped none of these women had heard about the Ghost Guide. Myths could be dangerous when they disappointed their followers. "Your sister, like all the other volunteers, experienced a metaphysical realm that is unreachable to most humans. How does someone describe seeing a color no one else has ever seen? As instincts and impulses took over, they felt as if they were being guided by some unseen force. It's not surprising that this compulsion was eventually personified. The 'Ghost Guide' is simply part of the transformation."

The petulant redhead didn't look convinced. "For Jillian's sake, I hope you're right."

The crowd seemed reluctant to disperse, but Lily wasn't sure what else to tell them. She gave Sara a quick hug. "I'll let you know as soon as I learn anything new."

Arton took Lily by the hand and led her off the ship. The sun felt wonderful on her face and her steps slowed. He didn't rush her. She tilted her head back and just soaked in the warmth and freedom. A gentle breeze stirred the trees and carried the scent of some exotic flower. She smiled. Wasn't everything exotic on an alien planet?

"That's the second time it's come up. Do we need to tell Kage about this Ghost Guide?" Arton asked once they started walking again.

"It's a myth," she insisted. "It's overwhelming for humans to experience the things Rodytes take for granted. Like yesterday when you showed me that creature in the woods. It's still hard for me to believe those images were real, much less that you put them inside my mind."

"Karrons," he muttered distractedly. "She called them karrons."

She picked her way through the trees, fallen leaves crunching beneath her shoes. There was no path to follow and she had no real destination in mind. She just needed to be outside for a while. "Still thinking about your mysterious elves?"

"The vision was so intense. It's hard to believe it was a random echo."

"Maybe the karrons just wanted us to stop calling them creatures." When he didn't return her smile, she sighed. His mood had been dark and distracted ever since Stront and Jillian refused to take his warnings seriously. "The battle born do an in-depth orientation with every female before she's accepted into the program. It sounds like we need to work up something similar."

"I agree. I'll mention it to Kage, but he'll simply delegate it back to me, so I'll start putting it together." He finally looked at her. "It will give me something to do, other than watching you work."

"I don't understand why the overlord is being so stubborn."

"If I'd marked you last night, it's likely he would have disabled the bands. I still think his primary motivation is to ensure that we end up a couple."

The Rodyte sense of smell was much more sensitive than that of a human. And male Rodytes were even more sensitive than females. They could identify each other by scent and immediately know when a female belonged to someone else. So they "marked" their females with their scent, announcing to other males that she was taken. Lily understood the concept. The details of how it was done, however, she'd never explored. On the *Triumphant*, she'd remained completely focused on work to avoid thoughts of Jakkin. And since her capture, she'd been too busy fighting with Arton to think about mating rituals.

If she asked Arton about it now, she was inviting a demonstration. The idea was tantalizing. However, now was not the time nor place. Rather than find herself bent over the nearest fallen tree, she let the subject drop. "I don't know where I'm going. Can you get us back to the ship once my wanderlust runs its course?"

"I think I can manage," he said with a secretive smile.

His ability to project his consciousness must come in handy in all sorts of situations.

They hiked for a while in silence. Lily enjoyed the mild exercise, while Arton seemed lost in thought. An insect buzzed toward Lily's face, so she quickly waved it away. "Can you communicate telepathically?"

Most harbingers can.

He slipped the thought into her mind so skillfully that it took her a moment to realize he hadn't spoken the words out loud. "Can you teach me how to do that?"

He shook his head. "Telepathy can't be taught unless you're born with the aptitude for it. If I reactivate the link I used yesterday, you could speak with me mind to mind. But it's unlikely you'll ever speak with others."

She shook her head. "There's that brutal honesty again. You really don't like sugarcoating anything, do you?"

He brushed his knuckles against the side of her face while his gaze moved over her features. "You're brilliant and accomplished, not to mention beautiful. Can't you be satisfied with who you are?"

The criticism stung yet flattered at the same time. It was very confusing. "Isn't everyone obsessed with the things they can't have?"

"I'm obsessed with you." He leaned down, clearly meaning to kiss her.

She turned her face away, too annoyed to enjoy his antics. "For now. Once you've had me, the novelty will fade and you'll move on to your next obsession."

His gaze narrowed and he put his hands on her hips, pulling her even closer. "You seem to know me so well. How many female 'obsessions' have there been in my life?"

Tipping her head way back, she boldly met his gaze. "How old are you?"

"How old do you think I am?"

She shrugged. "It's hard to tell with a Rodyte."

"That's right. Rodytes have a longer lifespan than humans. We also age more slowly. I'm considerably older than you think

I am. But my age wasn't the issue. You made it sound as if I flit and flutter from one female to the next. How many males have you allowed into your bed?"

She didn't want to talk about her lovers. Only one had been important to her, and that relationship had ended horribly. The others were pleasant distractions, and she'd barely noticed when they moved on. "Four." She didn't elaborate, and he didn't press for details.

"I've shared pleasure with three females. I don't think either of us qualifies as promiscuous."

"I'm sorry." She reached up and rested her hands on his chest. "I didn't mean to insult you."

"I'm not insulted. I'm frustrated by your opinion of me. You seem to doubt my interest, and I'm not sure why." He raised one hand to her neck, curving his long fingers around her nape. "Have I failed to reveal how much I want you?"

She lowered her gaze to his chin, unable to speak candidly while his intense eyes bore into hers. "I don't doubt your desire. I'm afraid I won't be able to hold your interest."

"Why?"

How did he manage to expose all her vulnerabilities while keeping his carefully guarded? "It has happened before, *four* times before." She paused, making sure the meaning sank in. "I can attract men with no problem, but they never stay interested for long. I'm too 'absorbed in my work', too 'emotionally distant'." She quoted the two most common complaints.

"Then they are not truly committed to you. Any relationship takes effort and attention. If you found work more interesting than your male, he was not trying hard enough. These males were not worthy of you."

Heat swept through her with intoxicating force. She couldn't decide whether to shiver or cry. Her body decided for her. Tears blurred her vision and her lips trembled. She stubbornly blinked away the moisture and licked her lips. "I wish we were compatible," she whispered, unable to suppress the thought.

"As do I." The torment in his tone made her look into his eyes. He shifted his hand so he could stroke her lips with his thumb. "We cannot change our genetics, at least not enough to make us compatible. Still, that doesn't mean we can't love each other, and be happy with each other."

Her eyes widened and her jaw dropped. Did he just use the L word? She swallowed hard. "Do you love me?" her whispered question was barely audible, and her heart was beating so hard she could feel it all over her body.

He laughed and the tension popped like a fragile soap bubble. "I'm not sure what I'm feeling for you. I've never felt like this before."

Boy, could she relate. "If the pull is even stronger than this, it's no wonder the others can't resist their potential mates."

Both his hands pushed into her hair and his mouth settled over hers. Her head was already back, but she tilted it to the side as well, finding a better angle for their mouths. His tongue teased her lips, darting and licking before surging forward to claim her taste. Then he filled her mouth and enflamed her senses with slow, deep strokes.

She trembled as pulse after pulse of need assailed her body. She wanted this, wanted *him* more than anything past or present. He might not express it often, but he clearly cared for her more deeply than she'd realized. Her clothes felt oppressive and her skin felt tight. She wanted to be naked and filled with him.

Anchoring her head with one hand, he skillfully opened the front of her uniform top with the other. He cupped one of her breasts and she sighed, needing the pressure of his warm palm. With both his hands occupied, hers were free to roam. She untucked his shirt and slipped her hands inside. His uniform was fitted, so there wasn't much room until she followed his example and parted the front seam.

"We have to stop," he whispered against her parted lips, but his hand moved to her other breast and teased the nipple. "I don't want our first time to be on the forest floor."

She quickly looked around and pointed to a rock formation about waist high and relatively level.

He growled and ripped off his shirt, draping it over the rock before he drew her toward it. "Someone could find us," he warned.

"I don't care." She shrugged off her shirt and stood before him unashamed.

"Gods, woman, are you trying to kill me?" But he snatched her shirt off the ground and spread it on top of his. Then he grasped her waist and lifted her onto the rock.

She laughed, feeling rebellious and wonderfully naughty. "You should have taken my pants off first."

He glowered playfully. "This is why females are only allowed to wear dresses on Rodymia."

It had been the same on the battle born ships. "I was quite relieved when you guys disregarded that custom."

"It wasn't by choice. The only garments we can mass produce are the standard uniforms." Clearly bored with the topic, he pulled off her shoes and unfastened her pants.

She lifted her hips, allowing him to pull her last garment off. Sunlight filtered through the trees, but it wasn't half as hot as his gaze.

"You are so beautiful." He placed his hands on her knees and gently guided her legs apart.

Heat crawled up her neck and spread across her face as he looked at her entire body. It wasn't like she'd never been naked with a man before, but Arton was staring at her sex with obvious hunger. Excitement unfurled, fueled by her memory of Jillian and Stront. Was Arton remembering the scene? He knelt on the leaf-strew ground and she had her answer.

His hands moved to the underside of her knees and he spread her thighs even wider. She leaned back, bracing herself against the shirt-covered rock. She watched him closely, unable to look away despite her slight embarrassment. His expression was so intense, so serious.

He brushed one knee with his lips, and then the other. Tension coiled inside her, making her restless and hot. He continued his torturously slow ascent, alternating sides after only one kiss. Back and forth, higher and higher up her inner thighs. But when he finally reached his destination, he only pressed one kiss to her aching slit, then moved onto her belly.

An exasperated sigh escaped her and he looked up into her eyes. "What's the matter, love?"

She shivered. There was that word again. "You're teasing me."

"I thought females enjoyed being teased before the actual joining."

She dropped her head back and stared up at the sky. "You know damn well what you're doing, or *not* doing."

"Say it," he urged. "Tell me what you want."

She closed her eyes. "I want you to do what Stront was doing to Jillian."

"I'm sure he did all sorts of things. You'll have to be more specific."

She never talked much during sex. Talking about the acts was more difficult than doing them in most cases. But Arton's commanding tone—and the fact that he was camped out between her thighs—sent shivers down her spine. "I want your mouth on me." He pressed his lips against her belly and playfully licked her skin. "Lower." He moved down a millimeter and did it again. He knew she was embarrassed and apparently enjoyed her awkwardness. Stubbornness alone made her bold. "Push your tongue between my folds and find my clit."

He kissed his way back to her slit, then did exactly what she'd instructed and nothing else.

"Please," she cried. "Use your mouth to make me come." It wouldn't take much. She was teetering on the brink already.

His mouth pressed in closer and his tongue finally moved, circling the cluster of nerves until she moaned. The tension wound, compressing the invisible coil. Her thighs shook and she rocked her hips, unable to remain still.

The orgasm burst suddenly and she cried out. Hard spasms of sensation pulsed through her core, radiating out through her entire body. She came down slowly, breathless and dazed, but he didn't raise his head. Instead, he shifted one of her legs to his shoulder so he could use his hand. He slipped two fingers into her core, triggering little aftershocks. Then his hand was sliding back and forth while his lips launched a new cycle of arousal.

She seldom came more than once and the few times she had, it had taken forever. "Arton," she tugged on his hair. "I want you inside me."

He ignored her, continuing the rhythmic slide of his fingers and careful suction of his lips. Left with no choice but surrender, she relaxed as best she could on a rock in the middle of a forest. He'd give up when he realized...but her body came alive again, responding as it never had before. The second orgasm built gradually, which made the sensations much more intense.

She dropped her head back again and closed her eyes, concentrating on the staggering sensations. He suddenly shifted her other leg to his back as well and lifted her hips toward his mouth. Then his fingers pulled out and his tongue slid in. The utterly carnal act pushed her over the edge. She cried out again, shaking violently as the second wave crested. He kept the spasms rippling, drawing every last shudder from her before finally raising his head. His face was wet, but he didn't seem to care. His gaze bore into hers, silver phitons gleaming.

"I think I could live on your taste alone." He licked his lips to accent his claim.

"You're welcome to try. I'll be happy to feed you anytime you like."

He grinned, apparently pleased by her boldness.

With her legs still draped over his shoulders, he quickly unfastened his pants. Then he stood and her legs slipped down to the bend of his elbows.

She pushed up against the rock, wanting to see all of him.

"Shit," he muttered, then quickly righted his pants. "Get dressed. There's a problem with Jillian. As I feared, something went wrong."

Chapter Six

Arton peered through the observation window and seethed. The medical personnel had allowed Lily into the chaotic treatment area. He, on the other hand, would have been in the way, so they relegated him to the waiting area. He watched Lily like a hawk, cringing each time she moved to the far side of the treatment table on which Jillian sprawled. He could feel the tether stretching, testing its limits, threatening to shock them both.

He felt helpless and useless. What good was a harbinger when no one trusted his visions? Everyone expected irrefutable proof, not vague descriptions and supposition. But he couldn't give more than he was given. Often his visions were more impression than detailed images. He occasionally misinterpreted what he was shown, but in the past two years, to his knowledge, he'd never been wrong.

Kage stepped up beside him, inhaled deeply, then smiled. "I guess we don't need these anymore." And with a pulse of psychic energy, he deactivated the tether bands.

"Gods be praised." Arton ripped the offending band off his wrist and handed it to Kage. The overlord took it and tucked it into the pocket of his uniform pants. Lily was too busy to notice the change. She was deep in conversation with Dr. Foran.

"So what went wrong, and why didn't your power warn us."

"It did," Arton snapped, angry all over again. "I warned them! They wouldn't listen. Even Lily refused to back down. You're the only one who takes my visions seriously."

"Silly them," Kage said without humor. "I've benefited from your visions too often to brush them aside. Back to the original question. Do they know what went wrong?"

"They know what Stront told them, but they're looking for a scientific explanation for her symptoms."

"Which are?"

"She's unconscious, completely unresponsive, and they don't know why."

Kage shot him an annoyed look. "That's what the scientists know. What did Stront say is wrong with her?"

"He said the soul bond anchored perfectly, that everything was wonderful, but..." This part was so weird Kage might even disregard it.

"But," he prompted, sounding even more impatient.

There was no way to make this sound less bizarre than it was, so he just blurted it out. "The Ghost Guide never showed up to help her release his magic."

The overlord faced him, folding his arms over his chest. He looked anything but amused. "The Ghost Guide? What in blazes is a Ghost Guide?"

"According to Lily it's a myth. According to the volunteers on Earth, it's a benevolent entity that makes transformation possible."

"Why is this the first I've heard about it?"

Good question. Arton's first instinct had been to tell Kage, but he'd been so distracted by his desire for Lily that he'd let the impulse slip away. "That's on me."

"You're damn right it is." Kage was using his overlord voice. Never a good thing. "That's why you're going to contact one of your brothers and find out exactly what, or who, this Ghost Guide is. If we failed to protect Jillian, it's our responsibility to make things right. And I don't care who you have to interact with to make that happen. Understood?"

Arton glared mutinously, unable to make himself agree. The last time he'd seen Kaden and Dakkar Lux, he'd delivered ransom demands on Kaden's mate, and the last time he'd seen Sedrik, he'd kidnapped Lily, and thousands of other human females. A warm reception from any of them was seriously doubtful.

"You will do this, or you can find yourself another anchor," Kage told him, his tone soft yet menacing.

The ultimatum shocked Arton. Anchoring a harbinger was an honor many coveted. Because the link was empathic, any crisis involving the anchor often triggered the harbinger's visions. The anchor also had access to harbinger energy. They didn't take on harbinger abilities, but the highly concentrated energy enhanced any natural abilities the anchor already possessed. The one drawback was that the anchor had access to the harbinger's mind. The wrong anchor could make a harbinger's life a living hell. Kage had anchored Arton faithfully for the past twenty-three years. Arton couldn't believe Kage would threaten him with the link now.

"Fine," Arton sneered. "I'll contact one of the Lux brothers and find out what needs to be done."

Kage accepted the assurance with a tense nod and walked back the way he'd come.

Angry, and hurt, Arton turned back to the window. The scene seemed to be calmer now. Stront sat beside the treatment table, holding Jillian's hand. The poor male looked devastated. Lily and Dr. Foran stood a short distance away. Apparently, she realized the bands were no longer active. She stood at least twenty feet from the observation window. She made a bland gesture toward him and Foran nodded, then smiled at her. Arton's gut twisted jealously. Gods, how he hated those stupid dimples.

I wish we were compatible. Uninvited, Lily's whispered plea echoed through Arton's mind. Understanding swept over him like a landslide and he shook his head. "That diabolical bastard." Kage's threat hadn't come out of nowhere. The wily overlord was still playing matchmaker. An anchor bond was nonsexual, so Arton had never thought of its similarities to a soul bond before. However, they were many. Both bonds allowed two people to share thoughts and feelings. If Lily became his anchor, it would also bind her life to his. Like a soul bond, becoming his anchor would allow her to live longer and she'd be much healthier than any human was naturally. The only problem it didn't solve was children, but wouldn't the other advantages make that disappointment a little easier to bear?

She'd have access to his mind. His *memories*.

The realization brought him up short and deflated his excitement like a sputtering balloon. Sweet, innocent Lily would see all of the brutal things he'd done, all the blood he'd spilled, the innocent lives snuffed out because of him. And worse—at least for him—she'd see everything he'd endured at Harbinger Academy.

A hand gently touched his arm and he gasped, whipping his head around to find Lily standing at his side. "Wow. You're distracted. Where were you just now?"

He shook his head. One look into her guileless eyes and he realized the futility of Kage's suggestion. Nothing would make him subject this woman to the horrors of his past. "Kage was just here." She'd sense it if he lied. Lily was shockingly perceptive for a human.

"Okay. Was he just checking in?"

"Basically." He cleared his throat and shook away the last of his momentary dream. They'd have to settle for being lovers, and he'd find a way to make her content within the limitations. "I'll explain the rest, but how is Jillian?"

"In a coma," she admitted. "She's stable and there is still brain activity, but it's strange, sort of muted. I've never seen anything like it before."

He nodded. "I told Kage about the Ghost Guide and he didn't take it well."

She sighed and took a step back. "We will find a medical solution to Jillian's illness. Mystic mumbo-jumbo doesn't help."

Mumbo-jumbo? He'd never heard the term, but its meaning was obvious. And it nettled him. If the headstrong couple had paid attention to his mystic mumbo-jumbo in the first place, none of them would be dealing with all this unpleasantness. "I might be willing to let you try, but Kage wants us to exhaust all possibilities."

"Meaning?"

They both had a tendency to become less communicative when they were upset. But why was she more upset now than when she'd entered the room? The answer came in a sudden flash of insight. If the Ghost Guide—whatever or whoever it turned out to be—was able to heal Jillian, that would mean her injury or illness could have been prevented. But Lily had disregarded the Ghost Guide as a myth. The reasoning was convoluted, but the outcome was clear. Lily blamed herself for Jillian's condition.

Acting on impulse, he pulled her into his arms and pressed her face into the warmth of his neck. Her scent soothed him. Hopefully his would do the same for her.

"What are you doing?" Her voice was muffled against his neck, her warm breath teasing his skin.

"Comforting you." Not very well, apparently.

She eased back and smiled at him. "I appreciate the effort, but I'm not really upset. I'm tired and frustrated, but those are common states of being for me."

He opened his arms and held up both hands. "Sorry."

"Don't apologize. The gesture was sweet." She wrapped her arms around his waist and moved closer, but kept her gaze on his face. "What did the overlord mean by exhausting all possibilities?"

"He wants you and Lentar to pursue—"

"Lentar?"

"Your dimpled doctor."

"Oh, is that his first name?" He nodded and her smile broadened. "You're adorable when you're jealous. Did you know that?"

"And you're as distracting as hells' outer rings. Do you want to hear the explanation or not?"

"I do, and I'm sorry. My lips are sealed until you're done explaining." She ran her fingers across her lips as if she closed an invisible zipper.

Looking at her made his chest ache. She was so damn beautiful. And he refused to consider what her nearness was doing to other body parts. They *really* needed to finish what they'd started in the woods. "You and Dr. Dimples can work toward finding a medical solution, but Kage wants me to contact one of the Lux brothers and get the inside story on the Ghost Guide."

"I'm an insider," she objected. "I was on both the *Intrepid* and the *Triumphant*. I talked to dozens of volunteers about their experiences. There is no Ghost Guide!" She pushed off his chest and moved away.

"I know you believe that, but Kage wants me to verify. This isn't a personal insult. And trust me, talking to any of the Lux males is the last thing I want to do."

"You can't even say it, can you?" She sounded disappointed and he hated that sound. After a month of arguing with her, he was used to her anger and impatience. Her disappointment, however, dismantled his fiercest emotions and made him desperate to please her.

"Say what," he asked between clenched teeth.

"They're your *brothers*, Arton. Sedrik, Kaden and Dakkar share your blood."

He snarled, unable to help the reaction. "Now you sound like *her*." He spun on the ball of his foot and stormed out into the corridor, nearly trampling a passerby in the process. The young man scrambled out of his way at the last minute.

"I sound like who?" Lily persisted, all but jogging to keep up with his angry pace.

"Skyla, *their* mother. My father's Bilarrian whore."

"Wow." She shook her head and used that disappointed tone again. "I've never seen this side of you. I'm not sure I like it."

"Drop the subject, or you're going to see a lot more of it."

She followed him into the lift. He hadn't been sure if she would. They weren't tethered anymore. Why didn't she go back to her cabin? He wasn't fit company for anyone at the moment.

"I'm not afraid of you." She lifted her chin defiantly.

"You should be," he warned her, meaning it literally.

She didn't listen, clearly believing he'd do her no harm. Maybe if she saw just a hint of his true darkness she'd run back to the safety of her cabin.

The lift slid open and he grasped her wrist, dragging her along behind him. "You want to play, little human? We'll play. But don't say I didn't warn you."

He scanned open his door and shoved her inside. She shoved him right back as the privacy panel slid closed behind them. "Stop manhandling me."

"I can't manhandle you, sweetheart. I'm not a man." He fisted the back of her hair and crushed her lips beneath his. She made a startled little sound and tensed for a moment, then melted into his forceful embrace. He wanted her fear, needed her to pull away, not her surrender. Why wasn't she afraid?

Without releasing her mouth, he ripped her shirt open, and then her pants. She let him, kissing him all the while like his actions were ordinary.

He stopped kissing her and searched her eyes. All he saw was warmth and acceptance.

"Do I get to rip your clothes off too?" she asked when the silence became uncomfortable.

"No need." He took off his uniform with defiant movements, his gaze burning into hers.

She looked at him boldly, gaze moving everywhere with obvious interest. "You have an amazing body, Rodyte. We'll just have to work on your attitude."

After delivering another warning glower he figured she'd ignore, he tossed her over his shoulder and headed for the bedroom.

Lily laughed, enjoying herself immensely. Her entire day had been a roller-coaster ride. Why should this be any different? Arton clearly needed an outlet for his grief and bitterness. If screwing her brains out was cathartic, then she was more than willing to "play", as he had so aptly put it. Besides she was ready for a little sexual therapy herself. If friends-with-benefits was all they would ever be, she might as well take full advantage of the benefits.

He tossed her onto the bed hard enough to make her bounce. He really was in full-on caveman mode, yet somehow he made it sexy.

Ripping off her shoes, he tossed them across the room then tugged her pants down and off in one violent motion. "Is that the best you can do?" Knowing he would never hurt her made her feel powerful. And she knew it was true with every fiber of her being. Arton would never harm her. He would protect her at the cost of his own life, if that was what it took to keep her safe. He'd even tried to comfort her. When her grim, brooding harbinger thought she was upset, he'd tried to cheer her up. Arton might suck at expressing his feelings, but he felt things deeply. Maybe too deeply.

"You don't seem to want my best," he returned. "You want my worst."

"You might be right." She shivered, nipples already gathered into tight little peaks. "So do your worst."

He required no other invitation. Joining her on the bed, he opened her legs with his knees. She didn't stop him, but she didn't make it easy for him either. She understood how this worked. He needed to dominate her, show her who was boss. Her passivity seemed to frustrate him, so she twisted and bucked, swinging her hands as if she meant to slap him.

Easily catching her wrists, he pinned her arms to the bunk on either side of her head. A secret thrill raced through her body. She'd always wanted a lover who wasn't afraid to be a little rough, but she'd never been bold enough to suggest it. So many things sounded amazing in fantasies while in reality they didn't work at all. Well, the reality of Arton's aggression was even better than she'd imagined.

He shifted her wrists to one hand and caressed her breasts with the other. She jerked away from his touch, though she wanted nothing more. He ignored her feigned resistance and squeezed each mound, his gaze alight with appreciation. Then lightly pinched her nipples.

"Is that supposed to hurt?" she challenged. His next pinch made her gasp and sent sensations spiraling through her chest and abdomen. "Now that was bad." He did it again only on the other side and her core clenched in needful spasms. Her spontaneous groan was so loud it made him grin, not a pleasant smile at all.

"What's the matter, human? Does your naughty little body crave the dark?"

She pressed her lips together, not ready to admit how much these pleasures thrilled her.

He released her suddenly and rocked back onto his knees. He paused just long enough to touch her folds and ensure she was sopping wet. Then he caught the backs of her knees and spread her legs as far as they'd go. The tendons burned in protest, but she held perfectly still, afraid to move, even holding her breath.

After positioning himself at her entrance, he paused, staring deep into her eyes. "You're mine, Lily." He growled out the words, part vow, part warning. "Never forget it!" Then he slammed his entire length inside her with one violent thrust.

She cried out, overwhelmed by the staggering fullness. It hadn't really hurt. She'd been more than ready, but he was definitely bigger than—she pinched off the thought. The past had no place in this bed. She only wished he'd figure that out.

He slowly pulled his hips back, closely watching her face. "Are you all right?"

She nodded, soothed by the question. Even in his darkest mood, he hadn't lost sight of her wellbeing. She swallowed past the lump in her throat and whispered, "It's just a tighter fit than I expected." She was careful not to make comparisons. That would doubtlessly piss him off.

He shifted one of her legs to his hip and slipped his hand between their bodies. His ferocious expression remained, but his touch gentled. He caressed her now, where before they grappled. She'd enjoyed the more intense approach, but she needed this now.

Apparently sensing the shift in her mood, he lowered his mouth to hers. The kiss started out forceful, but soon softened too. She buried her fingers in his hair, almost forgetting he wasn't restraining her anymore.

The hand between their bodies, circled her clit, rapidly building her arousal as well as her restlessness. The fullness was amazing, but she needed movement too. She tried to rock her hips and he growled without releasing her mouth.

Be still, he whispered in her mind as if to ensure there was no confusion. *If you want me to move, then come.*

She stopped trying to control things and concentrated on their kiss and the rhythmic stroking of his fingers. Pleasure built, bubbling up inside her with surprising speed. She came faster and harder with him than she'd ever thought possible. It was as if she'd never done this before. Actually, she hadn't. Arton wasn't human.

He tore his mouth away. "You're distracted again." He drew back and carefully pushed forward. Her body was still fighting him, even though she was trying to surrender. "Look at me. Think only of me and how good this feels."

She raised her arms overhead, secretly pretending he still held her down. She imagined herself tied up, utterly at his mercy, and liquid desire rolled through her core.

His gaze narrowed, then a wicked smile bowed his lips. "You're broadcasting. Keep thinking thoughts like that and I'll be happy to oblige you."

She licked her lips, embarrassed to be caught thinking something so wicked. Still, she refused to regret even her darkest needs. Arton's intensity made her feel wild and reckless.

His weight balanced on his knees and she realized there were only two points of contact now, his fingers on her clit and his hard shaft buried deep inside her. It forced her to concentrate on what he wanted her to feel.

Tension gathered beneath his fingers as she stared into his eyes. His phitons brightened, shining like molten silver. Her body was his to command. She was a willing balm for his embittered soul. *Use me.* She wasn't yet bold enough to say the words out loud. Wasn't even sure if he could hear her. *Release your pain and let my body heal you.*

"Come for me," he coaxed, his touch growing more demanding. She wiggled a little and he caught the sensitive nub between his fingers. She immediately stilled and he carefully pulled on the nub, plucking it like an instrument string.

Her orgasm hit without warning, the contractions so intense reality blurred. She cried out sharply, arching clear off the bunk. Every rippling spasm was its own burst of pleasure. Her inner muscles stretched tight around his thickness, she realized vaguely. The fullness made everything more intense. A fresh deluge of moisture rolled through her core, allowing him to slide smoothly.

Finally.

He grabbed her hips and quickly established a rhythm that drove her utterly insane. She came again in seconds, shocked beyond words. He lowered his upper body, sliding his chest and belly against her with each powerful thrust. His face was still too far away to kiss, but this felt better, more intimate. She needed as much of him touching her as possible. She wasn't sure why. She only knew she craved the contact.

"Damn it," he muttered, jaw clenching. "I'm not going to last. This feels too damn good." A few strokes later he cried out, shuddering violently.

She felt his warm seed gush into her and shivered, nearly coming for a third time. She'd never allowed her partners to ride "bareback". It felt wonderful yet unfamiliar. That pretty much described this entire episode. Rodytes were disease free and pregnancy wasn't an issue because they weren't compatible. The unwanted thought was like a bucket of ice water. She sighed and turned her face away.

He wouldn't allow the retreat. Turning her face back around, he asked, "What caused the sadness in your eyes?"

"It doesn't matter. I'm just wishing for things neither of us can change."

He sighed and separated their bodies, sprawling at her side. "I wish we were compatible too, but wishing doesn't make it real."

"I'm aware and I'm not upset. It was just a passing thought." She rolled onto her side and pressed against his, using his shoulder for a pillow. "This was wonderful. Do you feel better? You were pretty grumpy when we started."

"Grumpy?" He laughed. "Is that what you call it? I was about ready to strangle you."

"I don't want to start another fight, but I have to say one thing on the subject before I let it go." *For tonight*, she finished silently. "If you're not comfortable talking to me, I'll deal with it. But you need to talk to someone. The bitterness is eating you up from the inside. Even a powerless human can see that much."

He looked at her, but the animosity didn't reignite. "I've lived with the bitterness my entire adult life. I wouldn't know how to begin."

"You begin by wanting it gone," she suggested carefully, not wanting to anger him. "I need to ask a question about the situation, not your past."

"All right."

"How will you contact one of the Lux brothers without revealing our location to the battle born?"

He chuckled, then shifted his gaze to the ceiling. "I didn't intend to use traditional lines of communication."

"Then how?"

"I'll visit one of their dreams."

"You're a dreamwalker?" She propped herself up on her forearm so she could see his face. "I read about them, but I've never met one."

He grinned but still stared straight ahead. "How would you know unless they told you?"

"Good point."

"And I'm not an actual dreamwalker. I can only interact with..." he sighed and admitted, "those with whom I share blood."

"So you could contact your father, but not your step-mother?" She regretted the question the second it passed her lips.

"Actually, I dream shared with Skyla once, but she was pregnant with Sedrik at the time. Just barely, but it was enough."

According to Lily's research, Skyla Lux had extremely strong psychic powers, so she likely had something to do with the dream meld too. Rather than risk annoying him, she kept to the subject at hand. "Then which one will you target?"

"I'll start with Sedrik. He's the battle born general after all. Everything that takes place in Earth-space falls under his authority."

She didn't miss the mockery in his voice. "And if Sedrik won't let you in, you'll try Kaden."

He nodded, then finally looked at her. "You were assigned to both of their ships. Did you know either of them well?"

She shook her head, but a guilty blush spread across her cheeks.

His gaze narrowed and his body tensed. "Why don't I believe you?"

She was foolish to admit what had made her blush, but she could sense his determination to know. "I didn't know either of them well, but I wouldn't have minded getting to know General Lux a little better."

"You had a crush on Sedrik?" He sounded *almost* amused.

She shrugged, trying to downplay the admission. "Every female in his orbit has a crush on Sedrik Lux."

Arton dragged her on top of him and arranged her to straddle his lap. "Put me inside you and ride me. Now!"

As penance went, this was not so bad. She lifted up and guided him back to her entrance. She was wet, in fact really slippery from their mutual pleasure. She carefully lowered herself onto his impressive length, groaning as he filled her completely. "Oh yeah," she sighed.

He steadied her hips but held perfectly still. "Ride me," he ordered with more urgency.

She closed her eyes as she obeyed, unable to watch the bitter anger resurge within his gaze. Why wouldn't he let it out permanently? She rocked faster, taking him deeper. Maybe if they did this often enough, the past would eventually stay buried where it belonged.

Chapter Seven

Needing the focus of deep meditation, Arton carefully disentangled himself from Lily's warm body and scooted out of bed. They'd spent the past five hours alone in his cabin, laughing and talking like old friends. They ate dinner practically naked, then shared pleasure for the third time. It was amazing how easily she was able to...light his darkness. The phrase sounded foolish even in his mind, but that was what she did. She radiated warmth, hope and happiness, and his anger and bitterness just seemed to evaporate.

She'd said the first step toward healing was wanting the bitterness gone. He'd never cared if he was bitter before. In fact, it worked to his advantage to stay angry all the time. But Lily shouldn't be burdened with a bitter, angry male. She deserved someone who could see the joy in life and make her laugh whenever she became discouraged. Someone like Dr. Dimples.

Arton tensed. Just thinking of her in the arms of anyone else made him aggressive. He had no idea why, but she'd accepted his claim and he was determined to keep her!

He couldn't think about this right now. Jillian's life was on the line and the transformation program was on hold until the Ghost Guide issue was resolved.

With his purpose renewed, he walked into the living room. He grabbed the uniform pants he'd discarded earlier and stepped into them. At times clothes were distracting, but right now being naked reminded him of the warm, willing female sleeping in his bed.

He moved to the far corner of the cabin, away from everything and sat down, facing the walls. His legs were folded in front of him and he closed his eyes, tuning out his surroundings entirely. The trance came quickly. He'd had decades of practice to perfect the technique.

Releasing his inner being, he drifted through the vast currents of time and space, allowing himself a moment to acclimate. His awareness expanded beyond corporeal senses, yet without sensory input it was harder to understand what he perceived.

Slowly, he summoned a detailed image of the *Triumphant* into his mind. The ship was massive, one of the largest and most sophisticated ships the Rodyte military had ever produced. Arton sensed the ship in the distance, the energy of thousands of lives pulsing with myriad emotions. Ambition and impatience wrapped around hope and wistfulness. Rushing. People spent so much of their lives hurrying from one place to another. He propelled himself toward the target, dreading what came next.

Sedrik, the oldest and most successful of the three Lux brothers. He was also the most like their father. They were both career military, patriotic and sanctimonious. But Kryton Lux had been elite, privileged and powerful, his success assured from birth. Sedrik, on the other hand, was battle born. He had fought, in fact, kicked and clawed for everything he'd ever accomplished. In a rare moment of brutal honesty, Arton admitted that there was much about Sedrik to admire.

There was also much to resent.

Setting aside both extremes, Arton focused on Sedrik without feeling anything at all. Strong features and a piercing gaze, stubbornness and ambition. It only took Arton a moment to lock onto Sedrik's signal. His energy pulsed with vitality and...contentment? Arton snorted. Who wouldn't be contented in Sedrik's life?

The fearsome general lay curved around Rebecca, his newly claimed mate. They were already asleep, thank the gods, but they radiated post-coital bliss. Rather than let their obvious happiness bother him, Arton focused on Sedrik alone. Sedrik's energy felt different than the last time Arton had touched his mind. Of course. They were bonded now. Apparently, she had succeeded in releasing Sedrik's magic.

The development gave Arton pause. Did he dare even try this then? Entering someone's mind without permission, even for a harmless conversation, was considered an assault by most societies. Sedrik was no longer latent. He'd only had access to his power for a few weeks, but many skills could be mastered quickly.

Frustration surged through Arton. It wasn't really like he had a choice. The Outcasts' new world was pointless without the transformation program. And despite Lily's logical explanation for the phenomenon, Arton thought the Ghost Guide was real.

Sedrik's mind was at peace. Why shouldn't it be? The bastard had everything. A successful career, beautiful mate, and supportive family. All the things Arton would never, *could* never attain. Rather than wallowing in self-pity, Arton channeled his resentment into determination and focused again on the task at hand.

Abstract and continually changing, Sedrik's dream was filled with color and light. Arton gradually sank into the scene, meshing and flowing with the vital energy until he incorporated himself into the surreal images.

Sedrik sat on a rocky outcropping overlooking the crashing waves of the Froxtar Sea. The silver-blue sky was filled with water-color clouds and brightly plumed birds. Behind him Lux Manor sat on a grassy hill in all its palatial glory, exactly as Arton remembered it from his youth. Were it not for the harbinger gene, all this might have come to Arton once Kryton Lux passed beyond. Instead, it would pass to his battle born sons, and Arton—like all harbingers—was expected to do without any form of creature comfort. A fresh wave of resentment threatened his concentration, but he stubbornly forced it aside.

He wanted to have this over with as quickly as possible, so he pulled his being into a concentrated column and formed a visual representation of his physical body. He wore a dark blue tunic and dove-gray pants, the traditional garb for male harbingers. The tunic was decorated with shimmering silver embroidery. His was intricate and elaborate, denoting his status as organic.

Sedrik hadn't reacted to his arrival. So, how to begin? He took a deep breath and spoke in a calm, clear tone. "I mean you no harm. I just want to talk."

Sedrik whipped his head around and fury ignited in his eyes. He vaulted off the rocks and dove for Arton. "You worthless son of a bitch! Where did you take the human females?"

He swung for Arton's face, but his fist passed right through the image. "Coward! Solidify so we can finish what you started on my ship!"

Knowing a physical confrontation would be self-defeating, Arton had planned it like this. "The females are safe," he stressed. "Every single one of them is unharmed."

"I don't believe you," Sedrik sneered. "Let me speak with Thea Cline."

Arton hesitated. Bringing an untrained mind into a dream meld wasn't easy. He wasn't sure he could accomplish it. Of course, he'd never admit that to Sedrik. "I can't trust Thea to behave. She's hotheaded and impulsive. Will Lily do?"

"I suppose."

Sedrik's gaze narrowed subtly and Arton felt someone push against his shields. But it wasn't Sedrik. How strange. "Back off your friend or I'm out of here."

"My friend?" He even managed to sound innocent, but the other being was still there, digging, burrowing with shocking tenacity.

Arton reinforced his shields, then sent out a pain pulse, dislodging the intruder.

Sedrik immediately reacted to the person's distress. His expression didn't change, but his mental focus shifted. It had to be Rebecca. "I can talk to your mate if you'd rather. She seems determined to contact me."

"Leave her out of this." Sedrik made it sound like a threat.

"Then back her off!"

The pressure abated and he no longer sensed the other presence in the meld. She was likely still there. Soul bonds were continually active. At the very least, she was sensing everything Sedrik felt.

"Bring Lily here. This conversation goes no farther until I have assurances that none of the women have been harmed."

Arton reached for her, but his signal wasn't strong enough to connect without breaking contact with Sedrik's dream. Damn it. It was dangerous to admit any sort of weakness to the enemy. But he needed this, all the Outcasts did. He couldn't let pride stand in the way of progress.

Despising each word as he spoke it, he said, "I must siphon energy from this meld to bring her here."

"Understood."

He pulled a steady stream of Sedrik's energy into his being, shocked by the concentration of the molecules. His gaze shot to Sedrik and the bastard grinned, clearly relishing Arton's reaction. He hadn't felt energy this alive since—he dream shared with Skyla! Understanding the cause now, Arton was amazed by the similarities. Sedrik might look and act like his father, but there was much of his mother in him too.

Feeling almost dizzy, Arton reached for Lily again. She stirred sleepily. *I need you to speak with Sedrik. I'm going to bring you to where we are. Don't struggle or I could injure you.*

All right. Her mind was still a bit foggy, which made his job easier.

Very carefully, he wrapped himself around her and drew her into the meld. She didn't resist in any way, and the infusion of Sedrik's energy made the maneuver almost routine. Remarkable. Clothing her in a standard uniform, he manifested her image so she could interact more easily with Sedrik.

She looked around, eyes wide with awe. "This is...amazing."

"Lily, are you unharmed?" Sedrik's tone snapped with authority and concern.

She shook away the haze and looked at the general. "Yes, sir. We've been treated well, all things considered. In fact," she glanced at Arton, then added, "many of the females don't consider themselves captives anymore."

"Do you?"

It took her much too long to answer, but when she did, her words pleased him.

"No, sir. I don't want anyone harmed, so I'm helping them with their transformation program."

Sedrik's features hardened even more and his lips pressed together. "Have you been claimed by one of them? Are you under the influence of bonding fever?"

Her sad little smile made Arton's heart ache. "I'm not compatible with any of the battle born. You know that, sir."

Each time she said "sir" Arton cringed. And knowing she was attracted to Sedrik made the deference even more annoying. "Are you satisfied? I'm about to send her back."

"Yes," Sedrik muttered begrudgingly.

Arton released his hold on Lily, steadying her precious being until she was back where she belonged. "We've run into a snag."

"Have you now?" Sedrik's lips curved in a humorless smile and he folded his arms across his chest. "Isn't that just too bad."

He didn't need to know all the details, so Arton got right to the point. "How do I contact the Ghost Guide?"

Sedrik shrugged, but cunning gleamed in his dark eyes. "Don't know anything about it."

Suddenly Rebecca appeared. Curly brown hair framed her flushed face and anger flashed in her green eyes. She faced her mate, fists planted on her hips. "Stop shutting me out! This concerns me just as much as it concerns you."

"I don't want him anywhere near you," Sedrik insisted.

"Well, it's not up to you." With the issue settled, at least in her mind, she turned to Arton. "How many transformations have you attempted? Was anyone harmed?"

Had he found a reluctant ally? He would take whatever help he could find at this point. "Only one and yes."

Her eyes filled with compassion. "How badly?"

He glanced at Sedrik before admitting. "The female is in a coma."

"Damn it." She turned back to Sedrik. "I could go—"

"Absolutely not!"

"But Lily said—"

"I don't care what Lily said," he shouted. "We are not going to assist those criminals in any way."

"Don't raise your voice to me! If human females are in danger, I'll do what *I* think is best." She harrumphed then took a deep breath. "Being that my mate prefers not to help you, I suggest you contact your mother."

Arton set his teeth and glared. "My mother has passed beyond."

"Sorry. Your step-mother." She made an impatient face. "Just com Skyla. I better not say any more or my mate will strangle me."

Sedrik had locked his hands behind his back as if he were still struggling to contain the impulse. "You've already said way too much and you know it."

"Com her," she urged Arton, then disappeared.

Sedrik started to say something then sighed and shook his head. He suddenly looked sad and tired. "Why didn't Kage ask to be included in our program. It was always intended for anyone battle born."

He seemed genuinely confused, so Arton answered honestly. "We wanted a clean break, no ties to anyone or anything."

"Yet, here you are, asking for help. Doesn't that amount to the same thing?"

His tone was less combative, so Arton just shrugged.

They stared at each other for a long time, both too proud to make the first move. Finally, Sedrik sighed and spoke in a fast, frustrated tone. "All the females in my life keep insisting that I need to forgive you. I doubt you'll give a shit even if I do, but here goes. This conflict has gone on much too long. We're your family. We want you back."

Something vague and nearly forgotten stirred in Arton's soul. Several sarcastic retorts popped into his mind. Instead, he shook his head and said, "It's better this way."

"That's nonsense and you know it." Arton thought Sedrik was finished, then he added, "Just remember we're willing, as soon as you're ready."

Before Arton could react to Sedrik's sudden attitude shift, Sedrik forced him out of the dream meld and back into his own body.

Arton woke up with a gasp, shocked and disoriented. When reality came back into focus, he was still confused. What did Skyla Lux have to do with the Ghost Guide? And when had Sedrik started caring about anything but his career? The answer was obvious. Rebecca. Sedrik's bonded mate was softening the general, balancing his ruthless ambition with compassion.

It wasn't too surprising. One night with Lily and Arton was feeling all sorts of emotions he hadn't experienced in—maybe ever.

"All the females in my life…" So it wasn't just Rebecca. Who else could affect someone as self-righteous as Sedrik? The second name was just as obvious. Skyla.

His father's war bride was the quintessential do-gooder. She hated conflict in any form and pursued peace with laser focus and stunning tenacity. She had been exasperatingly persistent down through the years. She followed Arton around like a shadow, finding him each time he relocated no matter how well he concealed his tracks. If he didn't resent her so badly, he might have been impressed by her drive and ingenuity. She'd made it her life's ambition to bring about reconciliation between Arton and the rest of his family. Kryton had stopped hounding him a long time ago, but Skyla just kept coming.

Arton pushed to his feet and shoved his fingers through his hair. He hadn't spoken with Skyla directly in years. She'd started sending messages through Kage, who found her determination endearing. Only Skyla Lux could charm an overlord.

"So did he tell you anything?" Lily stood in the doorway leading to the bedroom, wearing only one of his shirts. It was unbuttoned to her navel, displaying the inner swell of her breasts and her long, shapely legs. He'd spent much of the past few hours familiarizing himself with her soft body and she still took his breath away.

She'd asked him a question. Oh yeah, what had he learned in the meld? "He didn't cooperate, but Rebecca did. Sort of. She told me to com Skyla, but didn't explain why."

"Skyla. Your step-mother?"

"My father's war bride. She's not *my* anything."

She smiled. "You didn't call her a Bilarrian whore. That's progress."

He didn't comment. Instead, he crossed the room and took her in his arms. "Because we're not related by blood, I can't dream share with her. I'll have to figure out another way to contact her."

Lily just nodded, but questions shadowed her gaze.

"What do you want to know? You're clearly gnawing on something."

"I think I understand why you resent your father, but the Lux brothers weren't even born when..." She sighed and shook her head. "Never mind. I don't want to fight with you."

Feeling unusually generous, or maybe he just wanted to make her smile, he steeled himself for the telling and began, "They replaced me. I was so broken, so ruined by the time they helped me escape that Kryton slammed the door on the past and built a shiny new life with his Bilr—with his war bride."

Her brows drew together as she mined for implications in the few facts he'd just shared. "How old were you when they rescued you?"

"Nineteen. And Sedrik was born eight and a half months after I returned home."

"Sedrik is what, thirty-five." Her eyes widened and she looked almost horrified. "You're in your fifties?"

He laughed. "I told you Rodytes age differently than humans. I've expended approximately one third of my lifespan and so have you. Is this really what you want to talk about?"

"No. It just caught me off guard. I want to know whatever you're willing to tell me. I really want to understand why you're still angry after all these years."

Scooping her up in his arms, he carried her to the bed and sat down with her on his lap. Her nearness calmed him, allowing him to relate what happened without being sucked into the emotional sewer associated with the events. "They both claimed to love me, to genuinely want me home, but I could see it in Kryton's eyes. He was disgusted and disappointed in what I'd become. And each time he looked at Skyla and his perfect newborn son..." He let out his breath slowly, refusing to give in to the emotions churning inside him. "I couldn't watch it, knew it would be easier on everyone if I just left."

"I suspect they wouldn't agree, but where did you go?"

"I signed on with the first opportunity that took me off-world. They happened to be Parillian mercenaries. When their leader realized what I was, he made damn sure his men didn't abuse me. He befriended me and convinced me to use my visions to make his life easier. I stayed with them for almost three years."

"Did you have any contact with your family during that time?" She spoke with obvious care as if she was worried he'd lose his temper. Little wonder. Her concern was justified.

He shook his head. "We were continually on the move. It would have been almost impossible for them to locate me. This also kept me safe from the guild's hunters."

"Hunters? Harbinger Guild was hunting you?"

"Of course. I was a prized possession. They had no intention of letting me go without a fight."

She shook her head, clearly upset by the idea. "That's so wrong. I don't know what to say."

"That's why I say nothing at all." He hoped she would take that hint, but she didn't.

"Where did you go next?"

If she wanted a blow-by-blow accounting of his entire career, this was going to take hours. Keeping her close, he crawled onto the bed and propped himself up against the wall. She lay between his legs, her upper body semi-reclining against his chest. The position was intimate without being sexual. Too bad.

"Next came the Sarton Conflict," he told her when she stared up at him expectantly. "It was too bloody for the Parillians, but I'd acquired a taste for it by then."

She shivered. "You 'acquired a taste' for war?"

He shrugged, but her reaction concerned him. He didn't want to damage the fragile connection they'd barely begun to build. Still, her curiosity about his past was persistent. "It was the perfect outlet for my rage," he admitted, but said no more.

She milled that over for a moment in silence, then asked, "When and how did you meet Kage?"

Like the berserkers of ancient Earth, Arton had been so consumed by the carnage that he was barely sane by the time Kage found him. "I was bleeding to death and more than ready for it to be over when Kage literally tripped over my body. I'm still not sure why he bothered, but he carried me back to his ship and his medics patched me up. I was furious at first, not in any way grateful, but he gradually pulled me back from the abyss and helped me learn to be less self-destructive. He's been my anchor for twenty-three years."

"What's an anchor?"

Shit. He did not want to tell her about the harbinger/anchor bond. She was smart and perceptive. It wouldn't take her long to reach the same conclusion as Kage. He chose each word with the utmost care. "Harbinger gifts operate best when they're linked with someone strong and dependable."

"The information I read talked about harbingers needing a 'master'. It said harbingers require the steadying presence of an objective handler. Is it sort of like that?"

"It's exactly like that, but most harbingers nowadays prefer the term anchor to master."

"I would too." She looked up and smiled. "Kage is a good choice. I can't imagine anyone stronger. I don't know him well enough to say if he's dependable or not."

Arton exhaled. Thank the gods for small favors. She'd accepted his vague explanation. Or he thought she had until she asked, "What does Kage get out of it?"

The way she'd worded the question gave him an out. "He has access to harbinger energy. His abilities don't change, but he's able to...supercharge his gifts when he pulls energy from me."

"Cool." She yawned. "You two are really close, aren't you?"

"He's my mentor, best friend, and boss." He chuckled. "I guess that constitutes close."

"Have you ever...you know, crossed the line?"

Few were bold enough to ask the question, but he knew many wondered if they were lovers. "I have no sexual attraction to other males and neither does Kage, but you're not the first to have wondered."

"There's a tangible connection between you two that seems unusual. I guess, you just told me what it is. He's your anchor."

"Go back to sleep," he coaxed, stroking her hair.

"You should too. That dream meld had to have exhausted you."

Oddly enough he wasn't tired. And she was right, he should have been. Bilarri was the source of Rodyte magic. And Skyla was Bilarrian. Was it really surprising that she'd passed on highly concentrated energy to her sons? Arton tried not to react, but it was one more thing for him to envy.

"I have to figure out a way to contact Skyla without revealing our location."

"Why don't you go to her?" She yawned again, then turned onto her side and snuggled into the warmth of his body.

It wasn't a bad idea. But it would take three days to reach Rodymia and another three to return. And who knew how long to gain her assistance. Could Jillian wait that long? No, he needed something faster, more direct. His telepathic reach was insufficient to ping her, a telepathic tap that encouraged her to form the link. Damn it. He closed his eyes and cleared his mind. He'd meditate and hopefully, he'd think of something.

LILY SPENT THE NEXT three days in the lab frantically searching Dr. Mintell's notes. The male was an overbearing ass most of the time, but he was brilliant and kept meticulous records of everything concerning the transformation program on Earth. He had encountered all sorts of complications, especially in the beginning, but nothing that paralleled what was happening to Jillian.

"Take a break already!" Lentar insisted from the doorway. "I don't think you've moved an inch since the last time I checked on you." He'd insisted she start using his first name. Reluctantly, she'd obliged. Arton was already jealous of "Dr. Dimples". She didn't want to add fuel that that particular fire. "I'm serious. Get out of here for at least an hour. Go outside or something. Staring at the display isn't going to change what's recorded there. Mintell didn't run across this exact complication. We're on our own."

She knew he was right, but wasn't ready to admit that they were out of options. Jillian's condition had started to deteriorate yesterday, so Lentar put her in stasis. The move bought them some more time, but it didn't solve the problem.

Lentar walked up behind her and rolled her chair away from the workstation. Then he tipped it forward, forcing her to stand up or end up on the deck. She laughed. "All right. All right. I get the point. I'll go reacquaint myself with the sun."

Not in the mood for a bunch of gossipy women, Lily disembarked using the midship gangway on deck three rather than emerging through the commons. Every Rodyte she passed averted his gaze and nodded respectfully. The change was stunning. They hadn't openly ogled her before, but their interest had been obvious. Arton's scent protected her now. For better or worse, she was the Heretic's female.

A cool breeze blew her hair across her face as she stepped out onto the nested stairway. The structure was covered, but the sides were open, offering no protection from the elements.

The day felt almost cold after hours in a stuffy lab, but she didn't care. Lentar was right, she really needed a break.

Lingering on the top platform, she looked around. Her view was partially obscured on one side by the *Viper*, and by the *Nexus* on the other. But in the distance she could see a series of fields the Outcasts had recently cleared. Were they going to build something or...plant some sort of crop? The thought made her laugh. It was extremely hard to picture these battle-hardened mercenaries pushing plows. The ships could provide food for everyone as long as the generators were recharged once a year. She wasn't sure what they used to recharge them, but she'd heard the term repeatedly. Anyway, it would sure be nice to have fresh fruits and veggies once in a while.

Shrugging off her speculation, she started down the stairs. She hadn't seen Arton since breakfast that morning. He'd been particularly prickly today. She understood his frustration. He wasn't having any better luck solving his problem than she was having resolving hers. His psychic range simply wasn't large enough to contact Skyla and any traditional means of communication risked revealing the settlement's location.

Shouts and stomping feet drew her attention to the ramp near the bow of the *Viper*. A small swarm of armed Outcasts raced out, then ran right in front of her. They were headed toward the clearing surrounding the Wheel. She waited until the last male passed, then hurried after them. She didn't want to interfere in whatever this was or get in their way, but what the heck was going on?

The soldiers formed a wide ring, which had them pointing their weapons at each other. A few seconds later the rumble of engines drew her attention to the sky. A small commuter ship, roughly triangular in shape, seemed to float down from the clouds, its movements slow and precise.

The Outcasts targeted the ship, but held their fire. Kage, Arton, and a male Lily didn't know came running from one of the other ships. She hadn't seen them exit, so she didn't know which one. They were trying to keep the settlement's location a secret from everyone, so clearly this visitor was uninvited.

The ring of soldiers shifted, making room for the overlord and his two companions. Arton looked around as he moved into position on Kage's right. Was he looking for her? Their gazes locked for just a moment. He acknowledged her with a nod, then turned his attention back to the newly arrived ship.

Lily crept forward while staying well back from the ring of armed Outcasts. Others joined her, rapidly forming a curious audience for this strange confrontation. A small hatch opened and a ramp extended. Tension was palpable, and Lily found herself holding her breath.

Two burly males in green-and-gold uniforms marched down the ramp first. They took up a defensive position on either side of the ramp, then a female emerged. She was dressed in a dark blue power suit with a narrow skirt instead of pants. She moved with the regality of a queen. Her dark hair swept away from her face and into a simple twist at the back of her head. Lily was too far away to see her eyes, but her gaze moved immediately to Arton. How strange. Did he know this female?

"Have you lost your mind?" he snapped moving toward her with angry strides. "We could have shot you out of the sky."

She offered him an enigmatic smile. "I knew you wouldn't."

"That's not funny."

The comment confused Lilly even more. Why did he think she'd meant it to be funny?

"Does your *husband* know you're here?"

Lily's eyes widened and understanding slammed through her. She looked at the female more closely. Was this Skyla Lux? Did she know Arton was trying to contact her? How the hell had she found this place?

Kage stepped up beside Arton and bowed to the stranger. "Overlord Kage Razel. It's nice to finally meet you in person, Madame Lux."

She was! This was Skyla, mysterious mother of the three Lux brothers, former war bride of Kryton Lux. Lily shook her head, amazed. She was too damn beautiful to have three grown sons.

"Likewise, Overlord Razel." She smiled warmly. "You've been a great help to me more than a few times and I appreciate it very much."

"At ease," Kage called to his men, then swept his arm toward the *Viper*. "Let's get you out of the sun."

"In a moment." She turned suddenly and walked straight to Lily. Her eyes were vivid blue, ringed in blood-red. The combination was striking in such a delicate face. "You're Lily, aren't you?"

A tingle raced down her spine. "I am, but how did you know?"

Skyla's answer was preempted as a pack of karrons bolted from the trees and charged the crowd. Screams mixed with growls and feline roars. People scrambled, running in every direction, shoving and colliding in the confusion. The battle cats raced through the panicked mob, weaving in and out while snarling and snapping, flashing their razor-sharp teeth. Solders ran after the cats, desperately trying to lock in a shot that would hit nothing but the animals.

Skyla's guards hurried her back toward her ship as Arton fought his way toward Lily. She reached out a hand toward him when a searing pain stabbed into her thigh. She gasped in a breath as she looked down and screamed. One of the karrons had ahold of her leg. It tugged with all its might as if trying to drag her along with it.

Fight or flight engaged and she turned aggressive, beating the cat on the muzzle and head with tightly clenched fists. The battle cat barely noticed. Using both hands, she tried to pry its jaws open, freeing her leg, but only managed to trip herself in the process. She went down hard on her hip, then quickly covered her head with her arms as someone almost trampled her.

Her other leg was suddenly grabbed by two more karrons. Their aim was better than the first's had been. They mostly caught her pant leg and not her flesh. They were clearly working as a team. If her life weren't in danger, she would have found their behavior fascinating. Adrenaline sped her pulse and added to her strength. She clawed at the ground, and kicked wildly, desperate to slow their progress or dislodge them completely. Even if it shredded her leg, she'd still be alive. They drug her free from the crowd and headed back into the trees, their human prize trailing behind them.

Energy pulses arced through the air and pelted the karrons like painful rain. Their armor absorbed most of the energy, but they yelped and whined, sounding more like dogs than cats for a change.

All at once, as if hearing some signal, all three of the creatures opened their jaws and ran into the surrounding forest. Lily watched their retreat in stunned appreciation. Had they just responded to the pain or... She searched the shadows as she struggled to sit, ignoring the throbbing protest of her left leg.

A sudden movement drew her eyes to something—or someone—standing in the shadows. The person spun around, dislodging his or her hood as they ran deeper into the forest. Lily just saw them for an instant, but two things had been clear. They'd been wearing a hooded cloak, and they had strange silvery hair. Had she just seen one of Arton's elves?

"Are you all right?" Arton knelt beside her, fear contorting his features. He looked her up and down. "Shit, they really did a number on your leg." He carefully pulled her into his arms, then maneuvered to his feet.

"I'm pretty sure I can walk," she objected, but waves of pain and nausea were taking turns inside her. "It's an animal bite, not a plasma blast."

He didn't argue. He just carried her back toward the *Viper*, his long strides just short of a jog. "I've never been so terrified in my life."

She reached up and touched his face, pleased by the confession. "I'll survive. I promise. But I've never seen anything like that. If they'd wanted a meal, why didn't they just... That was organized behavior. They were—kidnapping me."

"They've only drawn blood three times and all three have been women," Kage added as he caught up to Arton. Apparently, he'd heard her musings.

Arton nodded. "They growl at males, but only attack females. It's all very strange."

"I saw someone in the trees," Lily explained. "I think she was—commanding them."

"She?" Arton and Kage exchanged skeptical glances then Arton went on, "Are you certain you saw a female?"

She sighed. "I'm not certain of much, but I saw someone with silver-white hair."

"It must have been a trick of the light," Kage dismissed. "Arton had me convinced he was onto something, but Torak just returned from his sweeps of the caverns. He confirmed that we're the only inhabitants on this planet."

So Warlord Torak was the other male who came running out with Kage and Arton. He was even taller than the overlord, and looked just as mean. She'd only seen him for a moment, but he left a menacing impression.

"Maybe his scanners can't detect this sort of life," she suggested. "Their fundamental molecular structure could be based on something other than carbon. Humans have long speculated that there might be silicone-based life forms."

Kage just shook his head. "Our scanners might not have been able to identify them, but they still would have picked them up."

He could deny it all he liked. Lily knew what she'd seen. There had been a silver-haired, cloaked figure in those trees.

Chapter Eight

A rton shot to his feet, no longer able to maintain his cool. "I will not share a meal with that female and pretend that we are friends!"

"No. You'll share a meal with her and *stop* pretending you're enemies!" Kage shot right back. He stood on the other side of a large, square table designed to seat eight. They'd retreated to the war room for privacy when Arton returned from the clinic. Lily's leg required regeneration, so she was sleeping off the sedative. "We need to know how Skyla found us," Kage went on, "and we need to know about this Ghost Guide nonsense. And you're going to find out for me."

Running both hands through his hair, Arton paused for a deep breath. "First Sedrik and now Skyla? If I didn't owe you my life, I might take this personally."

"You take everything personally," Kage countered. "That's part of the problem."

Arton just glared at him. The war room was adjacent to the *Viper's* command deck, which was where Arton had caught up to Kage. Even though the ship would likely never leave the ground again, each system needed to be monitored and maintenance. Without the ship's replication abilities, the living conditions would have been primitive indeed.

"Is Lily still sleeping?" Kage asked after a long, tense pause.

Arton reached for her mind, assessing her wellbeing without violating her privacy. "She's resting peacefully."

"Good. Have you told her about the anchor bond yet?"

Clenching his fists, Arton squared his shoulders and lifted his chin. "I see no need. Our arrangement has worked well for more than two decades. I don't want to change it."

"Then you're an idiot." There was no hint of humor in Kage's tone. "Lily is extraordinary. If you screw this up, I'll court her myself."

Arton searched his friend's gaze. Had he meant that literally? "She's mine," he growled.

"Then act like it. The anchor bond would allow you two to communicate like true mates. You could—" He stopped himself and waved away the rest. "I'm preaching to the choir. You know more about it than I do. It's the answer and you know it. Stop being such a coward."

"I am not a coward," Arton flared. "Lily is too…sweet to understand many of the things you know about me."

"That's horse shit and you know it. Lily is much stronger than you're giving her credit for. She wants to *mate* with you. You need to get her as close to that goal as you possibly can."

"I hear you." But he didn't agree to follow his advice. "I'll set up something with Skyla." Then he took the coward's way out. "As soon as Lily wakes up."

Kage finally chuckled. "Need a mediator? Or just moral support?"

"A little of both. I'll let you know how it goes."

Arton returned to his cabin and found Lily still soundly asleep. He changed out of his uniform and into a pair of faded jeans and a T-shirt. Nothing else felt as comfortable, in his opinion. He'd fallen in love with the human garments during a prolonged mission in Chicago. A team of Outcasts had been hired by government officials to secretly eliminate strategic gang members and drug dealers in the hopes of controlling the criminal activity in certain areas of the city. They'd eventually fulfilled the contract, but the strategy had only been partially successful.

He tossed the uniform into the recycler and the computer announced, "Skyla Lux would like to enter. Shall I let her in?"

"Sure, I've got nothing better to do." His sarcasm was lost on the computer, but it understood enough to approve the visitor.

He walked out into the living room as the main door slid open. Skyla had changed as well. She wore a casual dress with a full skirt, and her hair was now loose around her shoulders. "Why are you here?" Despite his promise to the overlord, he couldn't quiet summon civility.

"First hell hounds and now your hostility, you're not making me feel very welcome."

He smiled helplessly. She was just too damn likable. "They're called battle cats, and I've always been hostile, so why are you surprised?"

"Not surprised, just disappointed. I was hoping Lily would have you straightened out by now. How is she, if you don't mind my asking?"

It would have been more of a shock if she hadn't known about Lily. Skyla was the most powerful psychic he'd ever met and that was saying a lot. "Resting. Her leg required regeneration, but it responded very well. It will be tender for a day or two, but nothing she can't handle. So, what brings you to our humble settlement and how did you manage to find it?"

"Print me a glass of blood wine and I'll tell you."

Bilarrians and their blood wine. He grimaced. It might not contain actual blood anymore, but he had no desire to drink the stuff. Still, if she was determined to go through the motions, he was willing to play along. "Have a seat."

She strolled over to the sofa and sat, her skirt billowed out around her. He printed the requested beverage, handed it to her, then sat in one of the armchairs facing her. "How'd you find me?" So much for playing the attentive host.

After taking a sip of wine, she looked him in the eyes and admitted, "I tagged you when you first came home. I've been able to locate you whenever I want ever since."

Shocked and horrified he just stared at her. "You tagged me? Like an animal?"

"No, dear. Not a literal microchip. I imprinted your...how do I explain this? The rhythm of your energy is unique. I've used that uniqueness to search for you on the metaphysical plane. I've lost you from time to time—you've tried very hard to be elusive—but I always manage to find you again."

"Why? Why do you even care?"

She looked confused by the question. "I love your father with all my heart and your father loves you, even though you keep breaking his. I want to love you too, Arton, but you won't let me."

Arton pushed to his feet, unable to sit there and take her subtle attacks. "Kryton loved me so much that he left me in hell for nineteen years," he sneered. "Loving fathers don't abandon their children."

She shook her head and a weary sadness came into her eyes. He'd heard her excuses before repeatedly, but his instructors told a very different story. "Your father tried everything in his power to have you returned to him, but the law was on their side. A law that he has worked tirelessly to nullify, by the way. But when all legal recourse was exhausted, he tried to break in and steal you. Over and over, he tried. If he hadn't been a crown favorite, he likely would have been executed for his repeated attempts. How can you doubt that he wanted you back? He thought of nothing else."

Rather than echoing past arguments that had no resolution, he changed the subject. "Did Sedrik com you?"

With obvious reluctance, she followed his lead. "Not Sedrik. His lovely mate contacted me. Have you met Rebecca? I think you'd like her."

"I have met her and I do like her," he rattled off impatiently. "How much did she tell you?" If they kept this strictly business, maybe there was some tiny hope of success.

"One failed attempt, female is in a coma. Is that still true? Is there only one?" Clearly, she understood his strategy.

He nodded, momentarily unable to maneuver words around the lump in his throat. Why did her willingness to let the past drop bother him? He's the one refusing to talk about it. Gods above! These females were making him irrational. "Can you help her, or do you know someone who can?"

"I need to see her to decide."

"Of course, I'll take you to her."

Lily ducked back from the bedroom doorway as Arton and Skyla walked past. She didn't want to be caught eavesdropping. But what she'd heard tore at her heart. It was obvious Skyla was desperate for reconciliation, and equally obvious that Arton wasn't ready to try. Why did he have to be so damn stubborn? Sometimes she just wanted to shake him until his teeth rattled.

Once she was certain they'd gone, she pulled on the clean uniform Arton had left for her and went out into the living room. Maybe it was time to have a chat with Arton's best, and likely only, friend. She pictured Kage as she'd first seen him, chest bare, dark eyes flashing. The image still made her hands tremble, but she'd spent more time with him since then and he didn't seem to be as ferocious as his reputation. Or maybe he just knew how to turn that ferociousness on and off. Whatever the case, for Arton she would risk it.

She'd been injected with com-bots when she signed on with the *Intrepid*, so the language barrier that many of the former captives faced wasn't a problem for her. One of the main advantages of being able to speak Rodyte was accessing the ship's main computer. Her time on the battle born ships taught her all sorts of ship features that entertained and amazed the other women. She was about to utilize one of her favorites. "Computer what is Overlord Razel's current location?"

"Overlord Razel is in the war room. Would you like me to open a com-link?"

"That's not necessary. Is he alone?"

"Yes, Lily. Would you like an illuminated guide?"

That was the offer she'd hoped to trigger. She smiled and said, "Yes, please." A stylized star appeared on the floor, the symbol just bright enough to distinguish it from the rest of the decking.

Because all twelve ships in the Wheel were exactly the same, it was surprisingly easy to get turned around. The illuminated guide would escort her anywhere she wanted to go.

"Shall we begin?" The computer prompted when Lily didn't immediately start waking.

Did she really have the nerve to walk up to Kage Razel without an invitation and ask him to sit down for a chat? The knots in her stomach said no, but her stubborn heart shouted an emphatic yes. "I'm ready."

The illuminated guide moved slowly across the floor, only picking up speed when Lily walked faster. It led her out into the corridor, around two corners, and onto the nearest lift, which the computer activated without prompting from Lily. When they arrived on deck one, Lily hesitated. Was the war room restricted like the command deck? Only one way to find out. She took a small step forward and the star continued its trek toward the overlord's location.

When they reached an unmarked door, the computer told Lily to wait. She was starting to feel foolish when the door slid open and Kage Razel smiled down at her. "What a pleasant surprise. Are you looking for Arton?"

"No, sir. I was looking for you." She licked her lips, wishing she were wearing her lab coat. At least then she'd have somewhere to put her hands.

"Come in." He stepped aside so she could, then motioned toward the eight empty chairs surrounding the raised table. Eight rectangular screens were inset in the table, likely housing com-systems and holographic imaging. The war room was a fancy conference room, she realized, feeling a little less intimidated. "What can I do for you, and please call me Kage."

She sat on the first chair she reached. Like the table, it was raised, feeling more like a barstool than a conference room chair. Kage skirted the table and sat facing her. He was dressed in a uniform today. The sides of his head were completely shaved and the rest of his thick black hair—a five-inch patch down the center—had been combed straight back from his face. It was less dramatic than the Mohawk, but it made him look even more dangerous. The severe style accented the symmetry of his features and his magnetic eyes. "I...I'm not sure how to begin."

"I have an idea." He crossed the room and printed two mugs of something hot enough to steam. Returning to the table, he handed her a mug, then went back to his seat.

She raised the mug to her face and inhaled. The savory scent of coffee filled her nose and she closed her eyes and inhaled again. Then it dawned on her. "How did you print coffee? Everyone else thinks we don't have the molecular pattern for it."

"It's an overlord's prerogative to keep secrets, and to share them. Drink." He winked at her and Lily about dropped her mug. There was definitely more to Kage Razel than most people realized.

She took a long sip, savoring the full-bodied flavor. It was robust without being bitter. "It's good, really good."

"See, now we're just two friends having a cup of coffee. So tell me what's bothering you."

"You're best friend is driving me insane. He is filled with such pain and anger, but he also has his emotions locked down so tight, I'm not sure they can be pried loose."

"They need to be, badly."

With that one sentence, she knew she'd made the right decision. Kage was clearly an ally, so she poured out her heart to him. "First of all, I'm rapidly falling in love with him, which scares me to death. I want to help him, but I don't know how. He won't talk to me, won't let me do anything to comfort him. Well, other than...the obvious."

He smiled. "Sometimes the obvious can be very cathartic. Don't underestimate the power of sex."

Ten minutes ago she'd been afraid and now they were talking about sex. Go coffee. "I don't underestimate it and I'm not afraid to use it, but I need other strategies. I think it's going to take every trick in the book to penetrate his emotional armor."

"Undoubtedly." He slid his mug from hand to hand as he silently studied her. "Has he told you anything about his past?"

She hesitated. Was it disloyal to plot behind Arton's back like this? No. She had to figure out how to reach him and she was out of options on her own. "He's told me a little. Basically rattled off his resume. I know he's seen tons of battles and was exposed to everything that goes with modern warfare. But this goes so much deeper. It all started at the academy, didn't it? What did they do to him?"

"How much do you know about Harbinger Guild? Do you know how he ended up at the academy?"

She nodded, feeling sick already and they had barely begun. "He told me. But if he was a baby when they took him, did Arton even remember his father?"

"He was two, so it's doubtful. But other parents were allowed to visit. Arton kept waiting for his parents to return. Month after month, then year after year, he waited, hoping his family would be like all the others and take time to visit the academy."

"What kept them away?"

"The harbingers, of course. They claimed Kryton was dangerous, that he'd abused Arton before turning him over. None of it was true, but it was enough to get a court order preventing either of his parents from seeing him."

She furiously blinked back tears, feeling overwhelming sympathy, not only for the terrified child Arton must have been, but for his tormented father. It was much too soon to break down. They'd only covered how the tragedy began. She cleared her throat and gradually regained her composure. "Arton said there were laws allowing all of this. How the hell did that happen?"

"Harbingers predict the future, some with alarming accuracy. Ambitious people will do anything to access that sort of power. The guild leaders wanted to control anyone with even the potential for prophetic gifts, and greedy politicians were happy to oblige them. And the worst part was the harbingers began to prey on each other. The guild leaders were supposed to protect the trainees against exploitation and abuse. Instead they corrupted traditional training into something evil and auctioned the defenseless off to the highest bidder, regardless of the character of the person who won the bid."

"But all that has changed now, right?" She couldn't bear to think that children were still being abused in that horrible place. "There was a long series of articles about the reformation of Harbinger Guild."

"Yes. They're working very hard to clean up the mess, but that doesn't help Arton."

She drank some more coffee but it was really a stall. Did she want to know the specifics of what Arton had suffered?

"You need to know."

Her gaze flew back to Kage. Had he read her mind or just her expression? If she was serious about building a future with Arton, she needed to understand his past. Swallowing past her uncertainty, she said, "Tell me."

"As his anchor, I have access to his memories." Something almost calculative flashed in his dark eyes as he asked, "Has he explained what an anchor is?"

She nodded. "They used to be called masters, but anchor sounds less demeaning."

Kage hesitated, as if he'd say more on the subject. Instead, he sighed and returned to the overarching topic. "Their 'training' program utilized many brainwashing techniques, isolation, utter dependency, sensory deprivation, or over stimulation. He endured countless beatings. At times he was starved, and through it all, he was ridiculed and demeaned, told that he was nothing without his mentors. The guild was the only family he would ever have. He was so worthless, so hated, that his father begged them to take him away. Without the academy, he would be homeless and destitute."

Her first tear escaped with the sweep of her lashes, and then she couldn't stop. She covered her mouth with her hand and wept. "Who would do that to a child? God, who would do that to anyone?" Kage walked around the table and lightly patted her back.

After a long pause, he removed his hand and asked, "Can you take more or should I stop?"

She took a deep breath, then shook her head. "Don't stop. I want to hear everything."

"Not in one sitting you don't." He shuddered violently, then shook his head and walked back to his side of the table. He returned to his seat as he continued his explanation. "I've had more than twenty years to sift through his nightmares and there are parts I still can't stomach."

But Arton didn't have that choice. He'd lived through every horrific event. He had no way to escape the memories. "Go on."

Kage accepted her decision with a nod. "They convinced him he was a destitute orphan, when in reality he was heir to one of the largest fortunes on Rodymia. He was taught that his only hope in life was to hone his skills and dedicate himself to Harbinger Guild. Blind obedience and brainless acceptance was their goal with every trainee. So they played all sorts of head games with him. One tutor would be horribly abusive so another could rush in and rescue Arton from the abuse. This allowed the rescuer to gain his trust and take him deeper into the indoctrination."

"And this went on until he was nineteen?"

"He was rescued when he was nineteen, but he's still fighting to purge his mind of their...poison."

She nodded. They'd barely scratched the surface, she was sure, but it gave her a much better idea of what Arton had lived through. "And becoming a mercenary certainly didn't help in his search to find peace. Why couldn't he have become a house painter? I don't know, something soothing and mundane."

Kage chuckled as he stood. "Arton's search for peace is new, but I want to encourage it in any way I can."

"I agree." He was obviously ready to get back to work, so she stood too. "Thanks for the coffee."

"Anytime. And I'll offer one last piece of advice. Don't be afraid to push him. He's never going to bring those walls down on his own."

ARTON SHOVED HIS PLATE aside, not caring that his food was only half eaten. Listening to Skyla and Lily chat away as if they didn't have a care in the world had destroyed his appetite. Lily was clearly in awe of Skyla, and Arton couldn't really blame her. Skyla was impressive. Ten minutes after she'd walked into main medical, Jillian was sitting up fully conscious and joking with Stront, her newly bonded mate.

When Skyla was bombarded with questions about how she'd done it, she just smiled and said, "Trade secrets. I'm not allowed to say."

Kage drew Arton aside and urged him to question her in private. If they could learn how Skyla had freed Jillian from her mental oblivion, they should be able to prevent others from falling into the same trap.

So here he sat in his cabin's small dining room, sharing a meal with his father's war bride, the female he resented above all others. He watched her objectively, trying hard to keep his feelings distanced. Lily clearly found her amusing and warm. Even he had to admit Skyla was charming and undeniably intelligent.

"How did you do it?" he asked point blank as their conversation momentarily lapsed.

"How did I do what, dear?" Skyla looked at him over the rim of her wineglass. Her open, honest expression made her seem innocent, but the subtle hint of amusement in her voice told him she knew exactly what he was asking.

"How did you heal Jillian?"

"I'll explain it to you because you might actually understand my meaning. Those Rodyte doctors, even the overlord, have no real context for what Jillian was experiencing."

Most believed Kage was a techno-mage with no real psychic abilities, so her mildly bigoted conclusion didn't surprise him. "I appreciate your confidence. What happened to Jillian?"

"She was trapped on the metaphysical plane."

He nodded, remembering the images in his dream. "So you simply guided her out?"

"Basically. She had to free Stront's magic before the realm would release her, but that didn't take long once I calmed her down."

His gaze narrowed and he reached for his water glass. "Are you inferring that you're this Ghost Guide?"

She laughed and looked at Lily. "Took him long enough."

"But you were nowhere near Earth when the battle born transformations began," he pointed out.

Her elegant hand waved away his objection. "You can dream meld. You know the metaphysical plane has nothing to do with physical space. How did you contact Sedrik and Rebecca?"

"But why help the battle born? Their ambitions have nothing to do with Bilarri."

"I have little to do with Bilarri anymore. My life mate is Rodyte and three of my four sons are battle born."

Her four sons? Did she expect him to be flattered by the inclusion?

"One of your sons commands the *Intrepid*," Lily easily connected the dots. "Did Kaden ask for your assistance, or were you just checking up on him?"

"I was uninvited in the beginning, but it didn't take long for Kaden to figure things out."

Lily seemed satisfied with the answer, but he saw a hole in her explanation. "Their program is still going strong, and yet you're here with us. How are you able to accomplish both?"

"Delegation, silly man. I trained my replacement and she trained an entire team. The scientists can deny it all they like, but there is a metaphysical element to these transformations." She shot Lily an apologetic smile. "No insult intended."

"None taken. And I happen to agree. It's hard for we scientists to think outside the box, but it has become more and more apparent that there are forces at work in this situation that we can't explain through scientific principles."

"You're the Ghost Guide?" It made perfect sense, but his resentment made it hard to believe.

"Actually I *was* the Ghost Guide." She smiled again. "Rebecca now holds that title."

"Sedrik's mate." Arton rolled his eyes and pushed back from the table. "Of course he would find a female capable of commanding magic. Nothing but the best for good old Sedrik."

Skyla arched her brows, but sadness clouded her gaze. "Do you realize how jealous that makes you sound?"

"Of course I'm jealous of Sedrik," Arton snapped, yet he'd never admitted it before. Not even to himself. "Who wouldn't be?"

Skyla left the table as well, approaching him cautiously. "Your brother's life is pretty idyllic, but yours could be a lot better if you would stop fighting your heritage. You're a Lux, Arton. In fact you're—"

"I am Arton the Heretic! That will never change. Arton Lux died a very long time ago."

Skyla didn't argue with him, nor did she turn away. "Then how do I get to know the person you are now? I want to be part of your life and I'm willing to do so on your terms."

He just stared at her, unable to comprehend her motivation. She gained nothing by befriending him, so why make the effort? But evidence of her sincerity was all around him—had been for years if he were honest with himself. "Why?" His throat was so filled with emotion he barely got the word out.

She moved closer and tentatively touched his arm. "You know why. You're important to my life mate, which makes you important to me."

He ground his teeth and jerked away. "Only one thing is important to Kryton Lux and that is Kryton Lux. I need some air." Without looking at either of the females, he stormed from the cabin.

Chapter Nine

Torn between compassion and anger, Lily watched Arton stomp from the room. "He just might be the most obstinate person ever inflicted on this galaxy."

Skyla's smile was patient, almost serene. "You haven't met his father."

Lily pushed back from the table and put the dishes in the recycler, afraid she'd start throwing them if she didn't remove the temptation. "How can you keep doing it year after year? If someone slapped my hand away as many times as he's done it to you, I think I'd stop holding it out."

"If he were just being a jerk, I wouldn't put up with it. But Arton's resentment is born of pain, deep and abiding pain. The anger and bitterness has kept him alive. It's all he knows, all he has ever known."

"But he's safe now. Why can't he get past it?"

"I don't think he knows how." Skyla helped her clear the table, then they went into the living room and sat on the sofa. "He lashes out whenever he feels vulnerable. It's a protective mechanism and I'm not even sure he's aware of how often he does it."

"So how can we reach him without making him feel vulnerable?"

"I can't. Trust me. I've been trying for thirty-six years. The harbinger leaders convinced him that Kryton is a villain. Their lies penetrated so deeply that Arton believes them to this day. I'm an extension of Kryton, so I'm guilty by association. You, on the other hand, have no connection to my mate. You're part of Arton's new life, so there's a slim chance he'll let you in."

"I want that so badly, it's ridiculous." She sighed and whispered under her breath. "If only we were compatible. He couldn't hide from a true mate."

Skyla scrunched up her face, obviously confused by Lily's comments. "Aren't you his anchor? That's basically the same thing."

Lily looked into Skyla's eyes, intrigued by her statement. "What are you talking about? Arton's anchor is Kage, and Arton insists that they aren't lovers."

Skyla looked slightly guilty. "I think I've—how do you humans say—let the cat out of the bag."

"Well, the damage is done. You might as well explain what you meant. If you don't, I'll just ask Arton, and he's obviously not ready for me to know."

Pursing her lips, Skyla paused, likely debating her options. All of a sudden she shrugged and the tension melted from her features. "An anchor bond can be formed with anyone, so it can be nonsexual. However, if the harbinger wants it to be more, he can open the link so wide it rivals a mating bond. You would share thoughts and emotions, even experience life from each other's perspective once you learned to navigate the link."

"But it wouldn't allow us to have children together?"

Skyla shook her head. "Unfortunately not. To my knowledge there is nothing that can make that possible if you're not genetically compatible."

Lily nodded, saddened by the confirmation yet encouraged by the rest. If they could bond as closely as compatible couples, it would make life richer, more fulfilling. So why hadn't he at least told her it was an option?

"I shouldn't have said anything." Skyla frowned, compassion warming her gaze. "Clearly, I've upset you."

"No. Arton upset me. We've been together less than a week, but he keeps insisting he wishes we could mate. Either he was lying about that or... Is it possible he doesn't know about what you just told me?"

Again Skyla shook her head. "He knows. No one can construct an anchor bond without understanding how it works. I think he's protecting you from his past. If he made you his anchor—"

"I'd have access to his memories." Again Lily sighed, yet a bit of her frustration eased. It wasn't indifference that kept him away. It was his determination to protect her. "Kage told me he has a hard time coping with some of the images."

"Think how much harder it would be for you," Skyla cautioned. "You're not nearly as jaded as Overlord Razel."

"True, but that doesn't mean I'm too weak to deal with it." She loved his protective instincts. It made her feel special and cared for when he was ready to jump in and fight her battles for her. However, it also showed that he doubted the strength of her resolve. She straightened her back and lifted her chin. "Regardless of what Arton believes, I won't dissolve into hysterics if I'm exposed to the darker side of life."

"Males continually underestimate the strength and re-silience of females." Skyla reached over and squeezed her hand. "I do not. I know you can, and will, triumph over any adversity life sends your way."

"I appreciate your vote of confidence, but what I really need is a Ghost Guide. I assume you aren't willing to hang around until all the transformations have taken place."

Skyla's head dipped once acknowledging Lily's prediction. "That's a safe assumption. My mate will be furious when he re-alizes where I've gone. However, I will get things started like I did with the battle born. I'll spend some time with the trans-formed females and train a team leader."

"Who can in turn train her team of guides?"

"Exactly. I had an advantage with Rebecca. She bonded with my son, so her abilities mirror mine. Still, I'm confident I can locate someone equally competent. It's really not that hard once the person understands how to manipulate the metaphys-ical plane."

Lily knew her smile was wistful, but she couldn't hide her envy. She would never understand what any of it felt like unless Arton started trusting her.

Skyla suddenly turned her head toward the door, then gazed off into the distance. "He's on his way back." Her eyes re-focused and she pushed to her feet. "It's probably best if I'm not here when he arrives."

Lily stood too, fascinated by Skyla's casual claim. "You know where he is at all times?"

"Of course not. That would make me a god. I formed a con-nection to Arton years ago when we interacted in the dream realm. I'm able to sense him when his emotions are particularly volatile and when I intentionally search for him. It's not unlike the link I have with my biological children."

Something in Skyla's phrasing made Lily ask, "Do you consider Arton your son?"

"I always have and always will." Skyla's smile was sad as she headed for the door. "Now all I have to do is convince one of the most obstinate males in the galaxy to change his mind about me."

Lily followed her to the door, not wanting the visit to end. "Well, I won't just be rooting for you. I'll do everything in my power to help take the blinders off his eyes."

"I know you will." Skyla gave her a quick hug. "We'll talk again soon."

Arton returned so quickly after Skyla's departure that Lily wondered if they'd passed each other in the corridor. Rather than ask him about it and risk starting an argument about Skyla, she simply waited for him to speak. He made eye contact briefly, then strode across the cabin and manufactured a drink. After tossing back the cloudy blue liquor, he put the glass in the recycler and faced her.

"I can't be what they want me to be. I'm not sure I ever could." Rather than bitter, he sounded sad, so she didn't mention his rude departure earlier.

"What do they want you to be?" She moved toward him cautiously. His emotional volatility always made her feel helpless. "I don't understand your objection."

"They want me to be...one of them."

She wasn't sure what that meant. Only knew he believed it, and felt it was enough of an obstacle to prevent reconciliation.

"That might have been true in the past, but Skyla said she was ready to change. She said she'd do this on your terms."

He laughed, but the sound was harsh and humorless. "Why would Skyla Lux, cherished mate of the venerable Kryton Lux want anything to do with a renegade harbinger?"

As long as he believed that his father didn't want him, no one could convince him that Skyla's affection was real. They stood near the nutrition station, awkwardly facing each other. Less than four feet separated them, yet he had never seemed farther away.

Choosing her words with the utmost care, Lily ventured closer to the heart of the turmoil. "Can I ask a question without making you angry?"

His head tilted and his eyes narrowed. "If you have to ask, it's unlikely."

He was right, but she had to try. "Did your tutors ever lie to you?"

After a tense pause, he admitted, "Much, perhaps most, of what they told me was untrue."

She was so relieved that he'd answered honestly that she nearly lost her nerve. But this had to end, and their attraction gave her a freedom he would allow no one else. "Then why are you so certain that what your tutors told you about Kryton is true? Do you have other evidence that your father deserted you?"

A sound part sigh and part snarl escaped his throat as he skirted the table and chairs. He crossed the small living room and sat in one of the tall-backed armchairs. "I am well aware that the tutors played head games with me. Even before I had the freedom to research the validity of their claims, I suspected that they lied to me. There was one exception, however."

"Do you mean a subject or a source of information?" She followed him into the living room and sat on the sofa, which faced his chair.

"They were one and the same." He paused, taking a deep breath before he began. "Most of my tutors were vile, corrupt abominations. They controlled the trainees through fear and intimidation. Brother Nanteen was different. He brought me food and honest information, often at great risk to himself. To my knowledge, he never lied to me. And I verified his claims just like I verified everyone else's."

"It was this Brother Nanteen that told you Kryton abandoned you?"

He shook his head, face averted, gaze unfocused. He was clearly lost in yesteryear. "I was ten when I met Brother Nanteen, so I'd already been told that my *loving* father had no time for or interest in me. Kryton never even bothered to visit in over a decade. Not once!"

According to Kage, Kryton had attempted to visit numerous times, had exhausted every appeal and legal course of action, but the harbingers blocked him at every turn. Arton had doubtlessly heard the defense and rejected it, so Lily just listened.

"Kryton went on camera hundreds of times in a plethora of situations begging to see me or threatening Harbinger Guild." Arton's posture grew tense and defensive the longer he spoke. "He appeared heartbroken and tormented, but his pain was obviously a publicity stunt."

"A publicity stunt?" She tried not to sound as shocked as she felt. What the hell was he talking about? His conclusion didn't even make sense. "Kryton Lux was in the military. How does a general benefit from publicity?"

"Generals benefit from the support of rulers, and rulers benefit from publicity. Having one of the crown favorites all but martyred for such a sympathetic cause worked to the ruler's advantage. Harbinger Guild's leaders weren't showing the proper respect, so the ruler—with Kryton's assistance—pressured them to remember their place."

His explanation was so convoluted it made her brain itch. "How does Kryton pretending to grieve for his son pressure Harbinger Guild to 'show the proper respect'?"

"By sobbing pathetically and vowing to lay siege to the academy, Kryton created animosity against Harbinger Guild. There were protests and boycotts. They never lasted long or accomplished much, but the negative publicity was enough to curtail the bad behavior of the more rebellious guild leaders."

The cause and effect seemed flimsy, but he clearly believed every word. "You saw all of this as it happened, or you were told what was going on by your tutors?"

"I took nothing on faith. I knew my tutors misled and manipulated me, so I verified each claim with objective sources. Kryton used me like a prop for as long as it benefited his career, and then lost interest entirely."

It wasn't true. She knew in her heart of hearts that it was a reality the harbingers had shaped for him, but why did he defend it so vehemently? Why justify the actions of his abusers? "Who first told you this was happening? How old were you?"

He glared at her for so long she didn't think he'd answer. Had he simply tired of her questions or had she ventured too near something he didn't want to reveal? "The others claimed that Kryton abandoned me, that he dropped me off and never looked back. I knew that was unlikely. Pride alone would have demanded retaliation. But regardless of my protests and temper tantrums, my tutors wouldn't change their story."

"You didn't answer the original question. Who told you he was using you to further his career?"

"Brother Nanteen was the only person I trusted at Harbinger Academy. He was kind to me, protected me, so I asked him what was really going on."

"And he told you—"

"He didn't *tell* me anything. He brought me news feed clips and articles that documented Kryton's rise to power. As I said before, I saw much of what happened with my own eyes."

"You saw it happen live, or was everything provided by Brother Nanteen?" This was getting redundant, but she just couldn't give up. This was the first time he'd shared anything that happened at the academy. She would not squander the opportunity.

"I didn't attend the charity balls or council meetings, but the news feeds were live, or they were recordings of what had been live coverage." His gaze searched hers for a long moment before he asked, "What are you getting at? Just spit it out."

"Is it possible the information Brother Nanteen gave you was carefully edited so it told the exact story he wanted you to hear. Did you have direct access to any of the information or did everything come through the guild leaders?"

"You have no idea how long I fought against the conclusion that I meant nothing to my own flesh and blood." His voice grew louder as his agitation mounted. "Who wants to accept that about their father?" He shot to his feet, too angry to sit still. "I denied it and made excuses for him until it was obvious I was fooling myself." Pacing in front of the couch, he accented each point with a sharp gesture. "He used my image to garner support from all his rich friends. He spoke in front of the other guilds, trying to get them to denounce Harbinger Guild, yet he left me stranded in... Why didn't he protect me, if he loved me so gods damn much!"

She stood and cautiously approached him. The more vulnerable he felt, the more aggressive he'd become. She'd seen the progression, understood what fueled his fire. He wouldn't hurt her physically. Harming any female was unthinkable to him. But words could be just as hurtful as any blow. She had to remain strong, regardless of his bitter words or accusations. "He tried, Arton. It took him much longer than he wanted, but he never stopped trying."

His gaze iced over and features locked into an expressionless mask. "Change the subject or get out. I've lost interest in this conversation."

And already he shut down. Hurt and frustrated, Lily glanced at the door. If she left now, it was unlikely he'd ever allow her to return. He'd retreat deeper into his misery and reinforce the emotional barriers that needed to come down so desperately. Rather than attempt another direct approach, she shifted her focus and risked one last attempt.

"I'll never mention your past again—ever," she paused for affect. "If you do one thing for me."

His shoulders tensed and his features stilled, his gaze locked with hers. "Name it."

Her mouth dried out and her pulse raced. This was so reckless, so damn risky. The ultimatum she was about to issue might shatter the progress they'd made, but they'd remain locked in emotional limbo unless something she tried broke through. "There's no hope for our future unless we trust each other. I believe my actions and attitudes have proven that I trust you. Now I need a demonstration of your trust in me."

"Meaning?" He ground out the word as his jaw clenched.

"Make me your anchor."

"Absolutely not!"

Her heartbeat echoed in her ears, but she forced herself to throw down the gauntlet. "Then I'll walk away. Trust can't be one-sided."

He took an automatic step back, confusion clouding his eyes. Then understanding spread across his features. His lips pressed and his nostrils flared as he dragged his gaze from hers. "You don't know what you're asking."

"Actually I do. I know an anchor bond would allow us to communicate like true mates."

He snarled and turned away, his emotions setting him in motion again. "Who told you? Did Kage betray me?"

"No," she stressed, disappointed by every step he took away from her. "I spoke with him, but he was very careful not to violate your trust." Her admission seemed to fascinate him and she wasn't sure why.

He faced her again, though half a room separated them now. "You went to the overlord—a male that terrifies you—and asked him, what exactly?"

She swallowed with difficulty. He hadn't thrown her out yet. Was there some small chance he'd actually agree? "I asked him for advice on how to...get closer to you. I want—no, I need more than amazing sex from a long-term relationship."

He stalked toward her, stride rolling, utterly predatory. "And what advice did my best friend give you?"

Stubbornly holding her ground, she met his gaze. "He suggested I be patient yet persistent. He encouraged me not to give up."

A faint hint of a smile lifted one corner of his mouth. "You've got the persistent part down." They stood within easy reach of each other, but he made no move to touch her. "If it wasn't Kage, it had to be Skyla. She's the only other person with a full understanding of how the anchor bond works."

"She didn't mean to tell me. She presumed I was already your anchor, so my ignorance surprised her." Before he could respond to the statement, she asked, "Why didn't you tell me? You keep insisting that you would mate with me if you could, yet you intentionally kept this from me."

Something dark and dangerous sparked within his eyes. He raised his arm and wrapped one hand around her throat. He didn't squeeze, applied only enough pressure to ensure she felt the strength in his fingers. "You want to meet the real me? You honestly think you're ready for that sort of evil?"

"You're not evil. Evil things were done to you, but that doesn't make you evil."

"How would you know? You've never seen real evil." He lowered his hand to her shoulder, but didn't retreat. "Last chance, silly human." He raised his other arm and unfastened the top button on her dress. "Lift the ultimatum or I'll give you exactly what you asked for."

She had to be brave, had to be fearless, or she would never reach him. Their relationship would remain superficial and meaningless. Being with him, yet remaining separate from him, would be worse than not having him at all.

"I'm not afraid." It was a lie and they both knew it.

"You will be. I guarantee it." With smooth dexterity and ruthless focus, he unbuttoned her uniform top and guided her arms from the sleeves.

She watched his face, gauging his reaction to her surrender. She made no move to cover her body, even when he tugged her pants past her hips, leaving her naked before him.

"On your knees." His voice was rough, emotionless. He was still trying to frighten her, to drive her away so he could lick his emotional wounds.

If this was the price for their future together, she'd pay it gladly. Her discarded uniform cushioned her knees as she sank to the floor. If he was trying to intimidate her, it wasn't working. She reached for the front of his jeans, but he grabbed her wrists and shook his head.

"Hands behind your back."

Fine. He clearly felt threatened by her ultimatum and was trying to regain control. Well, she didn't want to control him. She wanted to comfort him. She bent her arms back and clasped her hands, keeping herself in the awkward position. Then she licked her lips and looked at him, challenge burning in her eyes.

His expression didn't change, but his hands shook a little as he opened his pants and guided her onto his cock. The maneuver was telling. He hadn't moved his hips toward her. He'd brought her mouth to him. If she wanted him to accept her demand, she had to accept his.

One of his hands slipped into her hair as he rocked his hips. He pulled nearly out before thrusting deep again. She couldn't really move without risking her tenuous balance, so she kept her lips in a firm circle and sucked. He moved faster, rocking her slightly with his fervor. Fighting for balance, she moved her legs apart. Her precarious position made her feel out of control yet strangely exhilarated. She was freed by the intensity of his need for her.

His gaze bore into hers, a combination of anger and hunger twisting his features. "More," he growled out. "Take it all."

His next thrust bumped the back of her throat, threatening to gag her. She combatted his aggression with tenderness, swirling her tongue and sucking even harder.

He groaned and tossed his head, clearly lost in the pleasure. Moving both hands to her face, he held her head at the perfect angle for his urgent thrusting. He possessed her, claimed her mouth with unabashed urgency.

She reveled in the frenzy, empowered by his obvious need. Her nipples tingled and her core clenched, more than ready for their next joining.

As if hearing her body's invitation, he pulled out of her mouth and staggered back a step. His jeans sagged around his thighs, but otherwise he was still fully dressed. He pulled her to her feet, then led her to the side of the sofa, bending her over the padded arm. She put out her hands to prevent herself from face-planting on the seat cushions.

He didn't speak, did nothing to reassure her as he kicked her feet apart and thrust deep into her waiting passage. The sudden fullness dragged a gasp from her throat and his haste set fire to her smoldering senses. She felt uninhibited, bold as never before.

Tossing her hair out of her face, she arched her back and took him deeper. His ragged groan made her smile, so she tightened her inner muscles and rocked her hips. He might have controlled her in the beginning, but they were equal partners now. He grabbed her hips, moving in and out with punishing speed.

"Is that all you've got?" She tossed the taunt over her shoulder as she slammed her hips backward, colliding with his groin.

"You want more?" He grabbed her hair and pulled her head back and to the side. "You want all of me?"

"Yes!" She met him stroke for stroke, wild with the need to break through his barriers. "Give it to me."

He sealed his mouth over hers, the kiss savage. "Can't say I didn't warn you," he spoke the words against her parted lips, then his presence stabbed into her mind. Reality shattered as his energy saturated her senses and infiltrated her thinking. Rage, incendiary and endless, burned through her soul, destroying everything in its path. She panted, yet her lungs still burned from lack of air.

As quickly as the anger flared, it subsided. She hung, suspended in utter darkness, alone and terrified. She struggled, but she had no arms or legs. She screamed and screamed, yet no sound rang out. There were no physical sensations of any kind, just an overwhelming sense of isolation.

Just when the loneliness threatened to overpower her mind, pain burned away the darkness. Images formed within the shadows, growing more distinct with each breath she took. A child with silver-and-black hair knelt on a stone floor, head bent, hands bound to the wall in front of him. A Rodyte male in a dark blue tunic and pale gray pants beat the boy with a wide strap. The strap left vicious red welts on the boy's pale flesh. The boy jerked and twisted, screaming in agony with each impact.

"I think you're starting to like this," the male sneered, sadistic hunger burning in his eyes. "Guess I'll have to dig out my whip."

The scene faded suddenly, replaced by a dizzying montage of images and emotions. Each scene was more disturbing than the last, each emotion more heartrending. She was insulated by the sheer speed with which they flowed.

The child was now ten or twelve. He huddled in the corner of a stone chamber, naked and filthy. His knees were drawn up to his chest and he rocked, trying in vain to stay warm.

She saw him training with a different tutor, though the purpose of the lesson was unclear. Arton was dressed in a dark blue tunic and pale gray pants, his hair had been shaved nearly to the scalp.

"Concentrate, you fool," the tutor snarled. "This should be second nature for you."

When the verbal prompting didn't have the desired result, the tutor swung a willowy rod, striking Arton across the back of his thighs. Arton gasped, but didn't cry out as his gaze iced over with hate.

The image faded and a chorus of voices echoed from the shadows.

"You're useless!"

"Organic, my ass. Your control is pathetic.

"We've been through this a thousand times before. Get it right this time!"

"Elite piece of shit. No wonder your father abandoned you."

"Are you a mental defective? This should be easy for an organic harbinger. You're just being stubborn."

The transfer sped even further. She saw physical and emotional abuse in every combination imaginable. More beatings, starvation joined burns, sleep deprivation and endless demeaning reticule. Arton grew hard and rebellious, challenging his abusers at every turn. Their punishments grew dangerously brutal, and still he wouldn't break.

Then the images slowed, blurring as the connection refocused. Like a video on fast-forward, each scene appeared individually, yet none lingered in her mind. He was a young man now, late teens, his body lean and whipcord strong.

Hard, driving lust accompanied the first image, building steadily with each scene that followed. Shame tainted the desire, so she fought against the current, not wanting to watch his young body violated by those evil monsters. She'd seen so much already. She'd hoped that the universe had spared Arton the final indignity.

But the lust emanated from Arton not his tutors. Arton was the aggressor in each scene. Some images were clearly consensual, his partners every bit as passionate as he. Yet some of the females lay trembling beneath him, faces turned away, eyes tightly closed. A few even struggled, pleading softly while Arton held them down.

"Evil enough for you?" Arton's deep adult voice sliced through the memories, yanking her back into the present. He held her pinned against the arm of the couch. His cock was still hard deep inside her.

Panting from the emotional tempest, she could barely speak. "I don't understand. Who were they? Why would you...take them if they didn't want you to?"

He drew back, holding her firmly in place with both hands on her hips. "Because you're wrong. I'm evil!" He punctuated the claim with a violent thrust.

She smothered her cry, knowing he was trying to make her react.

"I'm a rapist and murder." He wrapped both arms around her, one around her shoulders, the other banding her waist. And his hips took on a fast, shallow rhythm that kept her senses simmering. "Still want your mind linked with mine?"

"Yes," she stressed, but her voice sounded much less certain now. "There's a reason for what I saw." She tried to look at him. He released her waist and turned her head back around. "There had to be a reason. You wouldn't harm a female on purpose. Tell me why."

With a frustrated growl, he rocked her forward until her feet no longer touched the deck. "My cock was hard so I fucked them, just like I'm fucking you!"

He drove into her over and over, jarring her body with each impact. She braced herself with her hands, keeping her face from rubbing against the seat cushions. If their minds hadn't been linked, she would have been horrified. But she felt the pain, the desperate need for understanding that threaded through every hateful word. Despite his superficial hostility, they were closer to a breakthrough than ever before.

Chapter Ten

A rton firmly held Lily's hips as he plowed into her trembling body. Why wasn't she struggling, or at least screaming for him to stop? He'd showed her his past and the damage left behind by his tormentors. He was twisted, ruined, wrong, and he could never be right again. But Lily hadn't reacted the way he'd expected. Instead, she'd defended him, refusing to believe he'd been responsible for what she'd seen.

His balls tightened with the need to spill. He should end this and get the hells away from her. But she was warm and willing, utterly surrendered. Shame curled up through him. She didn't deserve to be treated like a whore, to be used without thought or care. She was special, selfless and compassionate. So why was he driving her away?

He kept her positioned with one arm but freed his other hand. He briefly caressed her back while he regained control of his body. Once he'd backed off his need to come, he eased his hand around to the front and cupped her breast. Warm and soft, her curves soothed his raw emotions, muting the past. He focused on her arousal, rewarding her loyalty with pleasure.

Shifting his hand to the underside of her breast, he caught her nipple between his thumb and finger. She arched into his touch, increasing the pressure. He teased the responsive tip until it gathered into a tight little point, then he moved on, targeting the other side. Her skin was so silky and warm. He wanted to imprint the texture on his mind, superimposing the sensation over other memories.

She canted her hips, taking him deeper and drawing his attention to where their bodies joined. He slid his hand lower, easing it between the couch and her pelvis, sliding down until he cupped her sex.

Her folds were soaking wet and he could feel his shaft sliding in and out of her snug passage. The discovery thrilled him, appealing to the possessive side of his nature. Her body was his. Her passionate heart was open to him, and no one would ever take her away!

He held her like that for a moment, savoring the erotic connection of their bodies. She moaned softly, her hips wiggling helplessly. With her feet off the deck, all she could do was relax and take what he gave her.

Slick with her arousal, his fingers moved up and covered her clit. She tensed with his first touch, then groaned as he rubbed and carefully plucked, experimenting until he found a caress that made her wild. He synchronized each circular stroke to the rocking of his hips. Urgent hunger gradually burned through his self-loathing. Regardless of the irrationality of her willingness, this female was *his*. And he would do everything in his power to protect her.

"Mine." He flicked his middle finger back and forth, making her undulate with each firm touch. "Say it."

"Yours," she gasped out. "I'm yours."

Then her emotions swept into his mind, dragging a harsh gasp from him. She wasn't afraid, at least not in the way he'd expected. Her only fear was that she might not be able to reach him, to help guide him out of the darkness permanently. Like sunshine melting snow, her affection warmed and soothed him, easing pain so acute he'd forgotten what life was like without it. He couldn't understand her attachment, certainly didn't deserve it, but she genuinely wanted to be part of his life and to make him part of hers.

The realization sent desire surging through him and snapped the last of his control. He shuttled hard and fast, lost to everything but the pleasure. His balls grew tight and his mind buzzed, invigorated by her energy. He thrust into her one last time, coming in violent shudders. Pleasure spread through his entire body, stealing his breath and bleeding the strength from his legs. She pushed up against him, trembling, her inner muscles rippling around his shaft.

"Gods," he moaned, sucking in a breath. "That's good. So damn good." Sliding her backward slowly, he returned her feet to the deck but didn't separate their bodies. He eased out of her mind, however, not wanting to subject her to any more of his darkness.

She panted, silent and still, likely stunned from all he had shown her.

"Do you understand now?" He brushed her hair back so he could see her face. "Your life would be like that every day."

"I don't believe you." Her voice was barely above a whisper, but conviction strengthened her tone. "I think you were forcing me to look. If the link were active all the time, I'd learn to ignore the memories."

With an abrupt scoff, he stepped back and quickly righted his pants. "Good luck with that. Decades of training have allowed me to control my mind and I still can't 'ignore the memories.'"

She peeled herself off the arm of the couch and turned around. "That's because you haven't forgiven yourself for what those monsters did to you, or what they made you do to others." Her face was flushed, hair mussed, and she seemed to have forgotten she was naked. "It wasn't your fault. None of it was your fault."

"I never thought it was."

Her gaze narrowed, and then understanding overtook her confusion. She sighed and shook her head. "You blame Kryton."

She sounded so frustrated, he had to look away. "I did for years, but I've come to accept that the harbingers are responsible for their own actions. And I'm responsible for mine."

"I disagree." She waited until he looked at her to continue, "They manipulated you in the worst possible ways. You had no control over anything."

He just shook his head. Arguing with her was pointless. Despite the evidence to the contrary, she was determined to defend him. Her attitude was slightly irrational, so why did it make him feel all warm and tingly? The crazy human was making him irrational too.

"How did the last part happen?" she persisted. "Did they threaten you? Drug you?" The hopeful catch in her voice made her seem painfully naive.

"I was eighteen," he countered angrily. "They didn't need to do anything other than shove a naked female into my room." It was a lie and the words tasted bitter in his mouth. Why wouldn't she give this up? She deserved so much more than he could give her. His ruthless seduction of her was further proof that he didn't deserve her.

"But what did they gain by encouraging you to have sex with all those females? Was it some sort of reward?"

It was obvious she wasn't going to let it go until she understood everything, so he spoke in the most general terms possible. "Organic harbingers can only create children with other organic harbingers. At least that's what they teach at the academy. As with most everything my tutors told me, it proved to be a self-serving lie. Still, I didn't know that at the time."

Finally remembering she was naked, she picked up her discarded dress and slipped it on before responding. "They were using you as a—breeder, with organic females?"

She made it sound almost as disgusting as the reality had been. "It was even more twisted than that. Female organic harbingers are extremely rare, so the guild leaders were desperate to overcome the limitation. They made changes to my DNA that were meant to allow me to impregnate anyone. They failed. Despite my best efforts—and I was an eager accomplice—none of the females conceived."

She just stared at him for a long time, her expression tense, gaze searching. "But if what they told you wasn't true, what limitation were they attempting to overcome?"

He pushed his hand through his hair. With anyone else, he wouldn't tolerate this sort of interrogation. Why was he indulging her? "Their goal was more or less true. They were trying to make me compatible with any humanoid female. Their justification—that organic females were all but extinct—was just utter rubbish. They simply wanted their prize stud to be as productive as possible."

She knew his darkest secret, yet she didn't back away, didn't turn from him in disgust. What was wrong with her?

"Have you had your DNA analyzed since you left the academy?" she asked. "Maybe the changes they made can be reversed or modified in some way."

"Of course I did. I've seen the best physicians and metaphysical healers in the galaxy and none of them can undo the damage." He shook his head and scowled. "I am what the harbingers made me." The past tugged at his soul, making his chest ache. He'd never told anyone about this, not even Kage. So why had he told Lily? What was it about this female that made him want to bare his soul? "But it was all for nothing," he muttered, disgusted with himself all over again. "They failed. I failed. All the pain and humiliation didn't result in even one child."

"All things considered that might have been a mercy." She glanced away from him as she concluded, "It kept them from getting their hands on another innocent, like you." She looked into his eyes as she said the last phrase, almost daring him to deny it.

"I'm far from innocent."

"You were dependent on those creatures for everything—food, shelter, life itself. And you'd been subjected to years and years of their mind control. You had no choice but to cooperate." She let the statement hang there for a moment before adding, "It wasn't your fault."

Something inside him shifted. It broke open and bled. How could she still believe in him after everything she'd seen? He'd shown her their faces, the ones he'd held down while they sobbed and pleaded for him to stop. How could she still... Emotion burned in the back of his throat and excess moisture clouded his vision. He furiously blinked back the tears, confused by her reaction. And his. Was her blind faith someone refusing to see the truth, or did she sense his deception?

"Why are you still here?" he demanded. "Are you that big a fool? I'm not your only option. Go flirt with Dr. Dimples. He's..." *worthy of you*. Emotion paralyzed his throat and he couldn't speak the words. Even as his mind tried to do the right thing, to force her to see what was best for *her*, his heart screamed in protest.

"I don't want Dr. Foran." She moved closer, her expression cautious yet unafraid. "I want you, only you."

He shook his head. "You deserve better, more."

Her brows arched and challenge tilted her head. "More than a powerful harbinger? The overlord surrounds himself with the most skilled and fiercest warriors. What does Kage Razel see in you?"

Her determination eroded his arguments little by little, and each layer she peeled back made him feel even more exposed. "Kage feels sorry for me."

She made an impatient sound and moved even closer. "Maybe in the beginning, but he trusts and depends on you now. He's your anchor, for God's sake. Why would he subject himself to that if he didn't value you?"

He had no answer and it pissed him off. If she wouldn't respond to reason, there was only one other way to drive her off, to protect her from his selfish desires. He summoned his coldest expression, raising his chin so he looked down at her. "I was trying to be polite, but you won't let me. It's over, Lily. I've lost interest in you." She started to object, but he raised his hand, signaling her need for silence. "My affairs never last long. You amused me more than most, so I kept you around longer than usual."

Uncertainty finally sparked within her gaze. Damn the woman was stubborn. "I don't believe you."

"I'm sorry, but you should have seen this coming." Each word he spoke shredded his own emotions, but he had to do this for her. "I tried to warn you, but you wouldn't listen."

"Then why pretend to care for me? Why tell me you wanted to claim me if only we were mates."

"The answer is in the question. 'If only.' If by some miracle we had been compatible, I might have been tempted to change. But this was just an affair. Like any other." His heart thundered in his chest and controlling his features grew more and more challenging.

She fiddled with her dress, hands trembling. "I think you're full of shit, but you obviously need some space so I'll give it to you." She took two steps toward the door, then looked back at him. "When you've tired of this nonsense, you know where to find me."

And then she was gone.

And he was alone again.

"HOW LONG ARE YOU GOING to hide in here?"

Lily looked up from the datapad she'd been staring at sightlessly. "I'm not hiding."

Sara stood just inside the door to their tiny cabin. Lily hadn't heard her friend enter, had been lost in her troubled thoughts. Sara's face was flushed and determination made her dark eyes gleam. "You've been moping around for almost a week. If Arton means that much to you, go tell him to stop being an ass! We both know he loves you as much as you love him. I don't see why this is an issue."

"I never said I love Arton, and I'm pretty sure he doesn't love me. He was physically attracted to me, but that wore off quickly." Some small part of her heart hadn't given up hope, so she didn't sound very convincing.

"Wow, hon, you better not gamble with me. You've got a terrible poker face."

Lily set the datapad aside. Sara's no-nonsense style was particularly annoying in Lily's current mood. She'd expected Arton to blow off some steam, maybe work out his frustration in one of the training centers, then knock on her door contrite and ready to apologize. But five days had passed and he hadn't reconsidered. She'd been in the lab every day, so it wasn't like he would have had trouble finding her.

She knew Sara was trying to be helpful, but Lily was out of ideas. She would not beg a man, any man, to love her. She thought more of herself than being that pathetic. "What would you do? If a man told you he'd lost interest and you were being a fool. How would you respond?"

"But he didn't mean it," Sara cried, moving farther into the small room. "He doesn't feel like he's worthy of you, so he drove you away. Any fool can see that's his true motivation."

Lily threw both hands up. "So what do I do about it? I'm open to suggestions."

Gathering her long dark hair in one hand, Sara tossed it over her shoulder. Then she walked to the bunk opposite Lily and sat down. "Find out all the places he goes and keep turning up unexpectedly. Out of sight, out of mind. You need to force him to think about nothing but you."

Lily shook her head and sighed. "He's barely left his cabin in the past five days. It's hard to turn up unexpectedly when your target is a hermit."

"Well, crap. There has to be something we can do." Her lips pursed and her eyes narrowed as she searched for alternatives.

"I'm trying to think of something, but nothing seems helpful. He thinks he's being noble, that he's protecting me. I have no idea how to combat that." Apparently Sara didn't either because she didn't respond. Lily waited for a few seconds, hoping her friend would come up with a clever strategy. When Sara said nothing more, Lily changed the subject. "How are the orientations going? Did the outline I gave you help keep you organized?"

Sara hesitated for a moment, as if she wasn't quite ready to move on. "The outline was a godsend. Thanks again for working it up. And the classes are going really well. It's nice to finally have something to do with my days."

Lily nodded, understanding the feeling all too well. Now that she spent most of her time in the lab or in main medical overseeing the transformations, her days flew by. "Each class is taking, what, three days?"

"I've got it down to two. The first time around, I included too many details and everyone's eyes started glazing over. The second try went much smoother. Everyone seemed to like it."

"And how many are in each class?" Lily wanted to know.

"Twelve. I tried twenty the first time, but the question-and-answer session took four hours. Again, the second class worked much better."

"With twelve in each class it will take two hundred fifty classes to include everyone. Even if you do two classes per week, it will take over two years." Sara's startled look made Lily smile. "We need more teachers."

Sara nodded, her expression thoughtful. "I'll ask each ship in the Wheel to choose a teacher. I'll train them and then I'll focus on the *Viper* passengers."

"A much better plan."

"So, right back at you." Sara leaned back on her hands and crossed her legs at the ankle. "How are the transformations progressing?"

"Slowly," Lily admitted. "We have the same problem. With only one Ghost Guide, we can only do one transformation per day. Now most of the men are still locating or courting their potential mates, but we already have a huge waiting list."

"And I get asked about that every day," Sara said. "When is the overlord going to release the names of more compatible couples? The males are doing their best to find their matches on their own, but it's damn hard to sniff three thousand females."

Lily couldn't help but smile as she pictured numerous Outcasts methodically sniffing their way through the commons on all twelve ships. "I no longer have an inside source, but Dr. Foran said the overlord will release new names as new positions become available on the waiting list. It already has a hundred names on it."

"Transformation isn't the only reason the males want to locate their female." Sara shot her a meaningful look.

"I know. But as I said, I no longer have an inside source."

Sara's brows arched. "Maybe you should do something about that."

Lily ignored her. Until Arton emerged from his self-imposed isolation, there wasn't much anyone could do about the limbo in which he'd left her. "Hopefully, Skyla will train another Ghost Guide, or three, and we can speed everything up."

"It's so weird. You had me convinced the Ghost Guide wasn't real and then she just shows up one day. And now you're a true believer."

"Have you met her?"

"Madame Lux." Sara shivered. "I'm not sure I want to. What I've heard about her is pretty scary."

"She's a sweetheart," Lily objected. "You don't need to be afraid of her." Lily had spent most of her midday breaks with Skyla since her fight with Arton. Skyla was warm and charming, extremely easy to like.

"Is she as powerful as they say?" Sara uncrossed her legs and scooted to the edge of her bunk. "For that matter, is Arton?"

Lily's mind link with Arton, even though it had been brief, had given her a damn good idea of his power. "They're both extremely powerful. But—"

"They only use their powers for good?" Sara laughed. "Couldn't resist. I can't trust your opinion of either of them. You're in love with one and the other will likely be your mother-in-law one day."

Lily smiled at Sara's optimism, but uncertainty still simmered inside her. Locking horns with Arton had revealed his stubbornness. Nothing she could do would make him reconsider his position unless at least part of him was open to the change.

MUCH LATER THAT NIGHT, Arton tossed in his lonely bed, missing Lily more with every breath he inhaled. Her image refused to leave his mind. Even meditation made him ache for her softness and the warmth of her gentle smile. He never should have touched her, never should have tortured himself with a taste of what could never be. He loved her, had loved her from the first moment he saw her, which made him even more determined to free her so she could pursue the sort of life she deserved. The sort of life he couldn't give her.

He drifted in a half-sleep, somewhere between troubled dreams and taunting fantasies. Warmth touched his face, flaring and receding like the heat from a fire. Something soft and ticklish eased between his toes. The sensation was so strange that he wiggled his feet, trying to identify the cause. He looked down and found himself standing on a large, gray fur.

"Greetings, stranger. Do you have a name?"

Shocked and confused, he snapped his gaze upward and stared into the crystalline eyes of his dream elf. She sat in a tall-backed chair, pearlescent hair flowing over her shoulders. Her bed chamber gradually came into focus around him, massive fireplace at his back, bed on a dais to his right.

"Arton the Heretic," he answered automatically, feeling compelled to provide the information. This wasn't a dream meld, at least not the sort he instigated. He was awake. He could still sense his body lying in bed. And yet he was here, in her private bower as well.

"I am Isolaund Farr of the Sarronti." She pushed to her feet and approached him, her stride slow yet assured. "This planet belongs to the Sarronti. You are trespassing. Pack up your ships and leave."

"No one will believe me. All of our scans indicate this planet is uninhabited. Where are you? Can you appear to my overlord?"

"I've tried. Your mind is the only one open to me." Her head tilted, making the muted colors in her hair swirl hypnotically. "What is your homeworld? Why have you come to mine?"

"We hail from more than one planet," he explained, frantically searching his mind for her point of entry. How had she gotten past his shields? Even now, he couldn't sense her. He could see her, hear her voice, feel the heat of her fire and smell the smoke. Yet there was no trace of an intruder in his mind. It didn't make sense. "I'm Rodyte. My homeworld is Rodymia."

Her shimmering gaze narrowed as she studied him. "I've never heard of it. And your female? Is she Rodyte like you?"

"I have no female." *Not anymore.*

She scoffed, her hair whipping out as she spun around and returned to her throne-like chair. "It didn't seem so the other day when my battle cats tried to capture her for me."

Fury swept into his mind, burning away his curiosity and concern. "It was you that day in the trees. Why did you attack my mate?"

"I didn't attack her. My battle cats were told to fetch not harm. One misjudged his bite and he was punished."

"Fetch her for what purpose? What did you want with my female?" He clenched his fists taking a step closer.

"I wanted to get your attention. The situation veered off course unexpectedly, but it sounds like I succeeded." She made a dismissive motion with her hand and the firelight gleamed off her long, pointed fingernails. "I know she's fine, so temper down the indignation." She crossed her legs, pressing back into the chair. "Besides, I thought you didn't have a mate. *Not anymore.*"

Her mocking tone warned him that she'd effortlessly read his mind. Her dwelling had to be nearby. Her battle cats harassed their guards on a regular basis. Unless she had a way of transporting them from some distant shore, but why feel so threatened by the Outcasts if her people lived on the other side of the planet?

"The females in your camp look slightly different from the males," she went on. "Are they a different species?"

Why did she care if all she wanted was their departure? Maybe if he answered some of her questions, she'd answer some of his. "Our females are human. Their homeworld is—"

"Earth." She hissed, sounding like one of her battle cats. "We know it well. Humans are vile, deceitful beings."

If she'd been to Earth, why hadn't she recognized the appearance of the females? "Have you ever been to Earth?"

"I'm asking the questions, Arton *the Heretic*. We are reasonable, but we will not be ignored. How long will it take for you to dismantle that monstrosity by the river?"

"We have no intention of leaving this place. If you're serious about wanting us gone, come see us in person." He made the suggestion as challenging as possible.

"You have thirty days. If I show up in person, pretty boy, I will have an army at my back!"

Chapter Eleven

A rton clasped his hands behind his back, afraid he'd punch his best friend squarely in the face if he didn't see reason soon. "It was no empty threat, Kage. The Sarronti will attack if we don't relocate. The other planet was—"

"I am not abandoning an uninhabited planet because you had a bad dream!" Kage seldom raised his voice, but he was shouting now, had been shouting for the past ten minutes. They stood in the living room of Kage's cabin, both too wound up to sit.

"There is no other choice," Arton insisted.

"I need proof." Kage snarled then shook his head. "You said this wasn't a vision, that your abilities didn't engage."

"It wasn't. I don't know how she did it." He shrugged, hoping his calm would deescalate Kage. "Maybe Skyla can explain how it was done."

"Has Skyla seen the elf witch too?"

Arton sighed. This was the first time in recent years Kage doubted Arton's visions. But then, as Kage said, Arton's experience hadn't been a vision. Not even a dream really. How could he expect the overlord to accept what he was saying when he couldn't even define what had taken place?

"Isolaund has appeared to no one but me. Lily saw her that day in the forest. Does that help my credibility?" His credibility shouldn't need help. His warnings and advice had guided Kage for two decades.

"You think the cloaked figure Lily saw was this elf witch?" Kage managed not to sound dubious, but Arton still sensed his doubt.

"Isolaund admitted as much. She ordered her battle cats to capture Lily and bring her into the woods, but one of them bit too hard and Lily was hurt."

"The elf told you all of this?" And his skepticism bled through in his tone.

"Yes, sir." Arton ground out the title between clenched teeth. They should be packing up the ships, preparing for departure! "I wasn't dreaming and I have no reason to lie. I want a home of my own as much as anyone."

"Then why have you rejected your female?" Kage lashed out unexpectedly.

Arton just glared at him. What transpired between him and Lily was no else's business. He would not justify his decisions concerning her to anyone.

"I'll double the perimeter guards and we'll start fortifying the Wheel. Without tangible proof to explain my actions, that's the best I can do."

Preparing for a war they could easily avoid made no sense to Arton. Still, he understood Kage's position. The Outcasts were starting to settle into a routine. They'd established boundaries and made their surroundings functional, if not yet comfortable. If Kage uprooted everyone without tangible proof that his actions were justified, one of the warlords would challenge his right to rule. And the consequences of that could be disastrous.

"Understood," Arton grumbled and turned toward the door. "I'll keep searching for evidence."

"Back to Lily." The harsh snap in Kage's tone brought Arton to an abrupt halt. "Stop avoiding her. That's an order."

Slowly Arton turned around. The overlord had no right to interfere in his personal life, and his best friend couldn't issue orders. "I'm not avoiding her. Our affair is over. It's as simple as that. End of story."

"Bullshit. You think she's too good for you and it's really pissing me off."

Arton glanced at Kage, then away, unable to bear the compassion in his friend's dark stare.

"How many times do I have to say it?" Kage asked. "You did *nothing* wrong."

Arton swallowed awkwardly as he turned his head back around. "I've killed hundreds of people and reveled in the violence."

"Wiping out enemies within the context of war is not murder. As for enjoying it." Kage shrugged. "It's a risk for every soldier. Battle creates a powerful rush that can become addictive."

"I also forced those girls to—"

"You kept them alive long enough to be rescued! A rescue you arranged at great risk to yourself." Kage's compassion was now tinged with an intensity that kept Arton from looking away. "If you hadn't fucked them, each one would be dead. Harbingers don't make idle threats. They would have killed the females one by one and forced you to watch them die. I've seen a whole lot more than you wanted me to see."

Arton said nothing. His throat was too tight to speak.

"Knock this shit off and go claim Lily. You've tortured her long enough."

"I'm not torturing her," Arton finally found his voice again. "I'm freeing her to find happiness with—"

"She won't be happy with anyone but you. Stop lying to yourself!"

"Stop interrupting me!"

Kage crossed his arms over his chest, his glare now as heated as Arton's. "If I thought for one instant I could make her happy, I'd beat the shit out of you and go claim her myself."

The barb found its mark, sending surges of possessive fury twisting through him. "Stay away from her!"

"Why? You don't want her."

Unwilling to make this physical, and relatively sure Kage would win that sort of fight, Arton just clenched his teeth again and continued to glare.

"Are you really going to make me do this?"

He thought Kage meant beating the shit out of him, but suddenly he felt a stinging pressure inside his mind. "What are you doing?"

"Severing the anchor bond," he snarled, stalking toward him with menacing purpose. "I will *not* be linked with a selfish asshole!"

Pain stabbed into Arton's brain and he screamed, clutching his head with both hands. "Stop it! You can't..." He screamed again as the pain intensified, tearing, burning, ripping through his head and down his spine. "I have to..."

With stunning strength and determination, Kage did the impossible. Suddenly their connection, a link that had thrived for twenty-three years split in two, leaving Arton emotionally savaged. His knees buckled and his stomach heaved. He stared up at Kage, tears of pain and disbelief escaping the corners of his eyes. "Why?"

"You're blowing it," he said simply, as if that explained everything. "You should be linked with Lily, but you're too damn stubborn to admit it. Only something drastic is going to force you to see what everyone else on this planet can see. Now stop fucking around and go claim your mate. I've had it with you today." Then he picked Arton up by the back of his shirt and the waistband of his jeans and literally threw him out of the cabin. "Don't speak to me again until you've claimed her!"

And then the cabin door slid shut in Arton's face.

Stunned and horrified, Arton just knelt there for long pain-blurred moments. What in hells' outer rings just happened? His brain pulsed and his psyche felt ravaged. But more than the pain and disorientation was a horrible sense of isolation. He was alone, truly alone, for the first time in twenty years.

Why would Kage do this to him?

You should be linked with Lily, but you're too damn stubborn to admit it. Kage's angry words echoed, providing a harsh reminder of his motivation.

Was Kage right? Would she never find happiness unless he claimed her?

But he was so dark, so jaded, so moody.

She enjoys your darkness and she's often the only one who can pull you out of one of your moods. Suddenly his inner voice sounded just like Kage. *As for jaded? Aren't we all?*

Arton glanced at the door as he staggered back to his feet. There were a million reasons he wanted to be with Lily, but what did Lily gain by saddling herself with him?

A man who loves her and will always protect her, even from himself. At least his inner voice sounded like him again. *But she doesn't want to be protected from you. She wants you, and only you.*

He closed his eyes and leaned his back again the wall. His legs still trembled.

If she truly wanted him as much as he wanted her, why should he deny her?

Kage's door suddenly opened and Arton forced his lids apart.

"Can you walk?" the overlord asked, his expression all business.

Arton nodded.

"Then follow. We've got another visitor."

Being able to walk and match the overlord's hurried stride were two different things. Each jogging step jarred Arton's head and pain ricocheted through his body. "Go on." He waved Kage forward. "I'll catch up."

"On the river side," he pointed in the general direction but kept on jogging.

Arton slowed his pace, allowing his mind a few more minutes to recover. He concentrated on his breathing as he walked, hurrying as much as he dared. He stepped into one of the central lifts and muttered, "Deck one." The elevator sank with a smooth motion and he pinched the bridge of his nose, eyes squeezed shut against the throbbing pain.

The lift stopped much too soon to have reached deck one, so he opened his eyes to see why. Skyla and Lily joined him in the elevator and he couldn't help but laugh. "The universe is out to get me today," he muttered, resuming his earlier pose.

"Nice to see you too, dear," Skyla said, sounding amused rather than annoyed. "Is something wrong? You look terrible."

"Headache."

Without asking permission, she gently touched the side of his face. Warm, tingling energy pulsed into his brain, immediately soothing the worst of the pain. "Did Kage—"

"Yes," he said before she revealed the nature of his injury to Lily. The last thing he wanted was her pity. "Do you happen to know the identity of our visitor?" He blinked repeatedly, then looked at Skyla.

"I'm not sure how, but your father has located me." The lift door slid open and she rushed out into the commons on deck one. "I won't let him cause trouble. I promise."

He lightly caught Lily's arm before she could get away. "We need to talk."

She licked her lips, then raised her gaze. "Are you sure you're ready? I can't take much more of this."

"I know, and I'm sorry." He sighed and motioned toward the front of the ship. "This won't wait, but I'm ready to resolve our issues for good."

"So am I." Still she twisted her arm out of his grasp and hurried after Skyla.

Did that mean she was ready to forgive him or escort him to hells' coldest ring?

He took a deep breath and hustled toward the disruption. One calamity at a time.

Kryton's sleek fighter, at least four times the size of Skyla's long-range shuttle, hovered over the river. The ship's subtle vibration created ripples on the glassy water and external lights shone out into the darkness, creating an eerie glow around the ship. People streamed out of the Wheel, curious and alarmed. All the Outcasts were brandishing weapons, while the females approached with much more caution.

Kryton bio-streamed to the ground, surrounded by six of his guards. He wore body armor, as any good soldier would. But his head was bare, a telling indication that he didn't feel threatened by the situation.

Outcasts rushed forward, ready to confront the intruders. Kage raised his arm and made a fist, halting the would-be assault.

Ignoring everyone else, Kryton strode directly to his mate. His gloved hands wrapped around her upper arms and he yanked her up, nearly off her feet. "Have you been harmed in anyway, or was this folly of your own making?"

"My eldest son needed my assistance, so I—"

He swept her into his arms and kissed her into silence. "You scared me to death, female. Do not do it again!"

"I was never in any danger. I just didn't trust you not to tell Sedrik how to find this place." She paused until he returned her feet fully to the ground. "Have you tattled on me? Are battle born forces on their way?"

"Not yet, but I may yet change my mind."

Arton watched the loving banter between Kryton and his war bride turned mate. Their continual teasing and their obvious love for each other had fascinated him during his months in their household. Apparently, their relationship hadn't weakened in three decades. The realization filled him with wonder, and hope.

He looked at Lily. Was it possible he could find such a connection with her?

She was watching the older couple with rapt interest, her expression part curiosity and part longing. Apparently her mood was rather like his.

Not ready to tackle that particular mountain, he shifted his focus back to the older General Lux. It had been eleven years since he last saw his father and the years showed on Kryton's face. He didn't look bad, just older, and more distinguished, if that was possible. There were more gray streaks now than blue in his dark hair, but his eyes were still sharp and filled with love for his mate. He stood straight and tall with the square-shouldered posture of those who spent their entire lives in the military.

"Now that you've found me," Skyla teased. "What are you going to do with me?"

He picked her up and signaled his ship.

"Wait! I was kidding. You are not leaving without speaking to your son. Now put me down!" She smacked him on the shoulder and wiggled until he obliged.

"Will my son speak with me?" He glanced toward Arton, cautious hope flickering in his blue-ringed eyes.

Always in the past Arton had been the one to reject his father's outstretched hand. It was long past time for him to make the first move. Fortifying himself with a quick breath, he straightened his spine and walked up to Kryton. Arton's heart thudded wildly as he held out his hand. "It's been a long time, sir."

"Sir?" Kryton glowered. "Don't insult me." Rather than slap Arton's hand away, however, he pulled him in for a quick yet firm hug. "You look like shit, son. Have you been ill?"

The criticism was so unexpected, and such a contrast to the tender look on Kryton's face that it shattered what little remained of Arton's composure. He laughed, almost hysterically, then was horrified to hear himself sob. What the fuck was wrong with him? But he couldn't stop the tears once they broke free. Without an anchor to stabilize his emotions, Arton felt exposed, vulnerable as he'd never been before.

Kryton wrapped his arms around his son, shaking a bit himself. Soon Skyla joined the hug and Arton was surrounded with love and acceptance. He was supported—safe. He sobbed, unable to stop the torrent of tears and emotions gushing from his battered heart. All the years of bitterness and rage flowed out like pus from an abscess.

He purged the hatred and released all the anger, no longer needing their protection to survive. He couldn't move on, couldn't prove himself worthy of Lily, until he put the past in the ground once and for all.

The pressure gradually eased, leaving him drained and depleted. He felt empty, as if he'd been hollowed out by an overzealous surgeon.

Then a spark ignited within the void. If even Brother Nanteen lied and Kryton had actually wanted him all along, how could Kryton explain the news streams and interviews? There had been actual evidence to support Brother Nanteen's claims.

Arton took one last shuddering breath, then stepped back and wiped the last of his tears away. He was too exhausted to be embarrassed by his breakdown. Some things were unavoidable. He wanted this settled, needed to be free of the past so he could concentrate on his future with Lily.

"They showed me news files of you, interviews and documentaries," Arton began without introduction. "You preyed on people's sympathy to gain support for yourself and Pern Keire." Who was one of the most corrupt rulers Rodymia had ever produced. "How do you explain what I saw?"

Kryton took a deep breath, then glanced around at the crowd of onlookers. "Is there somewhere we can go? I'd rather not do this with an audience."

"Are you sure?" Arton sniped. "You seemed to prefer an audience from what I saw."

"Use the war room," Kage said sternly. "It's as close as you'll get to common ground."

Kage was right. Arton's cabin would make Kryton feel defensive and Kryton's ship would do the same to Arton. He accepted the suggestion with a nod, then swept his arm toward the ramp leading to the *Viper*.

Lily looked at him uncertainly as he moved up beside her. "There's no way Skyla will be pried from his side. I'd like someone there to support me." He held out his hand as his blood rushed through his ears. He was half afraid she'd refuse him.

Lily took Arton's hand without hesitation, thrilled to be included in his reconciliation. She'd never seen him like this, so open. Or so vulnerable. He looked as if he'd just fought the most demanding battle of his life. Maybe he had. This couldn't have been easy for him. She gave his hand an encouraging squeeze and moved closer to his side.

The war room was on deck four, adjacent to the command center. Kryton led the way. Apparently he knew the design of these ships, which shouldn't have surprised her. Most of the Outcast ships had been salvaged or stolen from the Rodyte military.

Kage didn't accompany them. After shooting Arton an encouraging look, he entered the command center instead.

The couples chose seats on opposite sides of the raised table. Lily tried not to fidget, but she honestly thought she was more nervous than Arton.

"So, let me have it," Kryton encouraged. Luckily, there was no condescension in his tone. "What did you see? Let me explain each situation from my perspective."

"All right." Arton sounded sincere, likely for the first time. "I only trusted one of my tutors and he was the one who showed me the video clips. The first was some sort of fund raiser. You told an audience of at least two hundred all the horrible things the harbingers were doing to me and all the other trainees. You claimed that the money would be used to wage a legal war against Harbinger Guild."

"There were several such events," Kryton admitted. "I'm not sure which one he showed you. You explained my motivation for doing them. What don't you understand?"

Arton tensed, but his voice remained calm. "If you 'waged a legal war' against them, why did nothing every change at the academy?"

"Because Harbinger Guild was feared and protected by very powerful people," Skyla told him.

"More powerful than a crown striate?" Arton challenged. "Wasn't Pern Keire more powerful than anyone else on the planet at the time?"

"Yes and no," Kryton countered. "He had the authority to close down the academy, but my influence over him only went so far. He allowed my 'pointless campaign', that's what he used to call it, because I amused him and won wars in his name. But the harbingers also assisted him. There was no way he was going to choose one side over the other."

"You honestly took them to court?" Arton's expression was so conflicted, she couldn't decipher his reaction.

Kryton looked at Skyla. "Eleven times?"

"Fourteen, love. And that doesn't count all the official complaints and requests for an injunction."

Arton looked from one to the other, his gaze filled with pain. "And the interviews? Why spend so much time in front of cameras retelling my pathetic story."

"The story of what they did to you was shocking and vile, but never pathetic," Kryton objected. "When it became more and more apparent that I would never succeed through legal channels, I waged a war of public opinion. It was slightly more successful yet ultimately failed."

Arton reached beneath the table, obviously searching for her hand. She quickly slipped her hand into his and tightened her fingers, offering support and encouragement the only way she could without a mental link.

"And still, nothing changed." Now Arton sounded pained. Was he remembering all the things he'd suffered, all the times he'd been told no one wanted him.

Tears stung her eyes, but she quickly blinked them away. Breaking down now would only make him feel worse.

"I never gave up," Kryton insisted. "When the public moved on to their newest cause, I planned the first of many attempts to rescue you."

"But it's hard to spring a surprise attack on a harbinger?" His voice was barely a whisper.

"Exactly." A long pause followed. "You know the rest. My final attempt worked, but by then they'd succeeded in turning you against me."

"Why did the final attempt succeed when all the others failed?" Something in Arton's tone told her he already knew. Apparently, he needed to hear it.

"Because of me," Skyla told him. There was no bravado in her tone or expression. It was a simple statement of fact.

"I knew the only way I would best them was if I used magic to combat magic. I honestly pictured some grand battle with fireballs and spellcasting, but that wasn't what happened at all."

"He never would have taken a war bride if he hadn't been desperate to rescue you," Skyla stressed. "He has always found the practice abhorrent, and was instrumental in having it outlawed."

"So you snatched a dream walker and she contacted me so I could plan my own rescue," Arton muttered more or less to himself.

The convoluted explanation caught Lily's attention. "How did you help plan your own rescue?"

"We connected in the dream realm," Skyla told her, "but because my dreams are also prophetic, the Arton I contacted had already been rescued. All he had to do was tell me how we'd done it."

Lily tried to wrap her mind around how that would have worked, but it just made her head throb. So she nodded, deciding she didn't need to fully comprehend everything they discussed.

Arton let go of her hand and folded them on the tabletop. "You have to understand how convincing my tutors were, how..."

Kryton reached across the table and covered Arton's hands with his. "I don't blame you for your attitude. I never did. You were what they had programed you to be. My only regret is that I wasn't able to deprogram you fast enough to spare you life as a mercenary."

Arton allowed the touch, seemed hesitant yet comforted by it. "Trust me, it wasn't just you I was running from. A battlefield was the only appropriate place for me those first few years. I was so filled with rage."

"Are you less angry now?" Kryton sounded hopeful.

"Much." Arton pulled his hand back and wrapped his arm around Lily's shoulders. "And I have two incredibly persistent females to thank for that change. Thank the gods I'm only responsible for one of them."

Skyla smiled brightly, clearly thrilled with the praise.

"So what should I do with my wayward mate?" Kryton glared at Skyla playfully. "How much longer is this adventure going to take you?"

"A month?" she proposed, turning her beaming smile on Kryton.

"Two weeks," he countered firmly.

"With a one week extension for especially good behavior."

Kryton laughed, the sound rumbly yet warm. "I'm pretty sure you're not capable of it, so I agree."

"Can you locate and train your replacement, or replacements, in just two weeks?" Lily asked Skyla.

"Not entirely, but once everyone has access to the metaphysical plane, logistics won't be a problem. Or I can go old school and use a holo-com."

"Only if Kage agrees to a detectible form of communication," Arton reminded. "That's rather doubtful."

She made a face. "Fine, we'll keep everything hush-hush."

Kryton shot her a warning look. "You expect me to keep this from Sedrik?"

"I would very much appreciate it if you did," Arton stressed. "The last thing we need is the battle born rushing in to rescue a bunch of females who no longer want to be rescued."

"Are you sure that's true of all of them?" Kryton asked carefully. "Or have they become cooperative because they all believe that returning to Earth is simply not an option?"

Arton squirmed as if his chair were suddenly uncomfortable. "A vote was taken, but returning wasn't an option at the time."

"Is it an option now?" Skyla pushed a little harder.

"It's not my decision to make," Arton said. "I'll have to ask Kage."

"With one com, I can make it an option," Kryton warned.

Lily braced for Arton's response. He never reacted well to threats.

"I'm aware," he said evenly. "And I will encourage Kage strongly toward offering to return any female who doesn't want to be here. But ultimately it's the overlord's decision."

"I think we should give Arton the same two weeks you've given me," Skyla proposed. When Kryton didn't immediately refuse, she looked at Arton. "You work on the overlord for the next two weeks, help him see reason. We'll reassess the situation before we leave."

"Agreed."

Everyone exhaled at the same time, then laughed at the reaction.

"Well, I feel better." Skyla scooted back her chair, then stood.

"I know this is only the beginning," Kryton said suddenly serious again. "But I'm really happy with the progress we've made."

"I am too." The two men stood and started to hug, but Arton held out his hand instead.

It was hard to be disappointed after everything he'd offered. Besides, Kryton didn't seem overly concerned. He shook his son's hand, then led his mate from the room, whispering something wicked in her ear if Skyla's throaty chuckle was any indication.

Arton took both Lily's hands and helped her slide down from the raised chair. "Can we postpone our talk until morning? I'm honestly struggling just to stay awake."

"Of course." She tried not to be disappointed. He had to be emotionally drained by everything that had happened. But then, he'd seemed exhausted before he encountered his father. What had transpired between him and Kage? She'd seen Arton heading toward the overlord's cabin on her way to share a nightcap with Skyla. "Are you okay? Kryton wasn't exaggerating. You look ill."

He started to say something, then shook his head. "I haven't been sleeping well. I hope that's about to change."

"I hope so too." They held hands as they walked down the corridor.

"Can I ask one more thing?" He sounded adorably unsure.

"Of course."

"Will you stay with me tonight? I won't do any more than hold you until we've talked, but I can't be without you right now."

Her heart gave a happy flip. He needed her, wanted her near him. That was a wonderful start. "I wasn't sure how to ask, but I was hoping you weren't going to send me back to my old cabin."

"Never again."

True to his word, once they reached *their* cabin he pulled her into his arms but didn't even try to kiss her. She snuggled close, thrilled to be back in his embrace, but secretly wishing he were a little less exhausted.

Chapter Twelve

Waking up with Lily in his arms was the sweetest sort of torment for Arton. He carefully shifted onto his side so he could study her lovely face. She looked so peaceful in repose, so innocent and trusting. He gently combed her hair back from her face with his fingers. The silky strands slid against his skin making him eager to explore.

She murmured sleepily and rolled toward him, pressing against him even more intimately. They were both fully dressed, but his body stirred, aching to join with hers. Still, he held back, not yet ready to indulge his need for his mate. They might not be true mates in the literal sense of the word, but their bond would be just as secure, just as lasting.

The coming conversation was too important to rush or confuse with sensual pleasures, so he slipped out of bed and showered, then printed a fresh uniform. He was an Outcast, an integral part of this community. It was past time he started looking the part.

She woke a few minutes later, rubbing her eyes as she sat up in bed. "What time is it?" she asked when she spotted him in the doorway.

"Not quite nine. Do you have a transformation scheduled today?"

She shook her head. "It's too hard on Skyla if we do more than three in a row."

"Has she chosen an apprentice yet?"

"I don't think so." Lily shook her head, swinging her legs over the side of the bed. "But she's going to have to choose someone soon if she only has two weeks to train them."

"True. What would you like for breakfast?"

She groaned. "I'm not sure I can eat. Can we talk first?"

"Why don't you take a shower and wake up. I'll order your breakfast while you get ready."

"All right. Something simple, like toast and scrambled eggs."

"Got it." He waited until she disappeared into the utility room before he dragged himself away from the doorway. Then he printed a clean uniform for her and placed it on the foot of the bed. Not wanting her food to cool, he waited a few minutes to print her breakfast, then waited in the tiny dining room.

She joined him a short time later, her hair damp, faced slightly flushed. Was the color from the heat of the shower or anticipation?

"So two weeks with your parents underfoot? How will you survive?" She smiled, clearly hoping he wouldn't be upset by the gentle questions.

"It has been a long time coming," he admitted. "I'm looking forward to finally developing my own opinions of them."

She nodded, then paused for a bite of fluffy eggs. "Has anyone heard from Rex Dravon? If Thea is his genetic match, I know he won't hurt her. But shouldn't they have been back by now? It's been over a week."

"That's not unusual," he assured her. "I'll ask Kage the specifics of Rex's mission if it will make you feel better."

"Hearing from, or better yet, seeing Thea, would make me feel better."

He reached across the table and placed his hand over hers. Awareness arced between them, electric and alive. "She'll be fine."

Suddenly a grin parted her lips. "We should probably be worried about Rex. Thea can be hell on wheels when she's riled."

She ate for a few minutes in silence, then pushed her plate aside. "All right. I ate, like a good girl. Can we talk now?"

"Here or in the—"

"I don't care. Just talk to me. Tell me what you're thinking, feeling. I hate not being able to sense you."

Like a true mate would. She didn't have to say it. He saw it in her eyes. "The first thing I need to express is an apology. I've been really unfair to you and I'm profoundly sorry."

She accepted his statement with a nod, but didn't reply.

"It all started feeling really...real." He couldn't come up with a better word, so he moved on. "I was scared. I admit it. I expected you to run for the hills after the memory transfer. I didn't know how to react when you didn't."

She switched to the seat next to him and reached for his hands. He welcomed her gentle touch, hungry for any physical connection with her.

"I knew from the start that you'd suffered some sort of abuse," she began. "It was obvious you were lashing out. Learning the details silenced my curiosity and allowed me to focus on your recovery. Nothing you showed me changed how I feel about you. I'm not sure anything ever could."

He shook his head, struggling with a lifetime of insecurity. "It's really hard to believe that you care for me at all, much less can accept everything I showed you."

"You're not that hard to love, Arton. Or you wouldn't be if you'd forgive yourself and live in the present."

"I'm trying," he insisted. "And you make the effort worth-while."

Her smile was still a touch hesitant, but her gaze was warm. "So, where do we go from here? How do we make this relationship as harmonious as possible?"

"I take you to bed and make you my anchor." He held his breath as he waited for her reaction.

She didn't jump for joy as he'd hoped she would. Instead she released his hands and pressed back into her chair. "What made you change your mind?"

If he told her what Kage had done, she'd think it was the only reason he wanted her now. Still, he wasn't going to lie to her. Trust was impossible without honesty. "Kage has always been your most vocal supporter. He's threatened to claim you himself several times if I don't do it first."

"So you're protecting me from the overlord?" Challenge shaped her expression rather than amusement. He still had his work cut out for him.

"That's not what I meant. Kage is convinced you won't be happy with anyone but me."

"And what do you think?" Obviously, she wasn't going to make this easy.

He stood and pulled her to her feet. "I happen to agree with him. I don't understand why, but my darkness appeals to you. I don't have to pretend to be something I'm not with you because you love me just the way I am. You have no idea how comforting that is to me."

"Don't let it go to your head," she chided, meandering away from the table and heading for the bedroom. "There's still plenty of room for improvement. But you're right. I won't try to change you. I'll just support whatever changes you decide to make."

She was clearly ready to play, but he pulled her to a stop. "Will you explain why you're drawn to me? Do you even understand it yourself?"

"I'll do my best to explain *if* you'll be honest enough to admit why you hurt those girls. I know there was a reason."

That was no more than fair. Compromise was the cornerstone of successful relationships. "The guild leaders threatened to kill them," he told her, relieved to finally have it all out in the open. "If I didn't try to impregnate them, the guild leaders would have slit their throats one after another and forced me to watch them die. I figured the females would rather be alive and ravaged, than dead. I tried very hard not to hurt them, but frightening them was unavoidable."

She nodded, apparently satisfied with his explanation. "Do you know what happened to them?"

"They were rescued a few months before me."

Her gaze narrowed. "Did you have something to do with that?"

Even without an anchor bond she was too damn perceptive. He'd never be able to hide anything from her once they bonded. Not that he wanted to try. Part of the appeal of having a mate was being close enough to someone to want to share everything with them.

"I played a small but important part," he admitted. "I felt it was the least I could do."

"And the entire guild has been reformed now?" she persisted. "None of this is going on anymore?"

"Correct. The female who led the guild back then is dead and the entire council has been replaced. The new guild master is moral and just, at least by reputation. I've never met him, but my brothers have and they seem to like him." She caught his wrist and pulled him into the bedroom. It was exactly where he wanted to be, so there was no reason to resist. "Your turn," he reminded, not quite ready to oblige her. "What draws you to me?"

"My life is regimented, analytical—boring! You're challenging and mysterious, not to mention powerful in the magical sense of the word. I think it's as simple as opposites attracting. You are everything my life lacks and more."

"And if I become less challenging and mysterious? Will I be too tame for you then?"

She laughed. "I've felt your spirit, shared your emotions. You will never be too tame for me."

"Glad to hear it, because I'm done talking."

She grinned from ear to ear. "Glad to hear it, because I am too."

They stood beside the bed, kissing and caressing as they undressed each other. For the first time, their joining wasn't fueled by anger or pain, so they were able to take their time and fully explore each other. He lingered over her breasts as she tried to rid him of his pants. Her frustration was distracting, so he parted the seam and shed the garment with a few quick movements.

Once they were naked, they crawled onto the bed together, lying on their sides as they continued to kiss. He wanted to make this good for her, to prove that he could be tender as well as aggressive and wild.

She suddenly tore her mouth away from his. "Can we form the link now? I want to feel you inside and out."

He grinned with wicked intention. "There's more than one way to accomplish that."

"I want to feel what you feel as you push your cock deep inside your mate for the first time," she clarified in a sexy whisper.

Desire, hot and demanding, clenched his gut and made his already aching shaft buck against her belly. "It will hurt less if you're good and distracted while I anchor the link."

She returned his smile, her expression easily as wicked as his. "So find a way to distract me."

Unable to resist the challenge in her tone, he pushed her over onto her back and covered her with his body. He pinned her hands to the bed and kissed her deeply. "Are you sure this is what you want? Humans aren't used to having other people in your minds. The continual input can be—"

"I want this." She stared deep into his eyes. "I want all of you."

Then all you shall have. She couldn't hear his mind voice yet, but the promise echoed inside him. He would share himself without reservation, offering her everything.

After one final kiss on the mouth, he trailed kisses down her neck and across her shoulders. His tongue trailed along the ridge of each collar bone before moving on to her lovely breasts. They were firm and round, not large but nicely shaped. And her dark pink nipples responded so readily to his every touch, every lick or suck. He moved from one side to the other, then back, never getting enough of her softness.

She was shifting restlessly and arching her back by the time he continued his downward exploration. Her belly quivered and his torso wedged open her thighs as he settled on his knees between her legs. She was methodical and reserved so much of the time. Her freedom in bed always surprised him. It didn't seem to matter how demanding he became or how forcefully he took her. She was always responsive and selfless with her responses. Well, it was his turn to give. His turn to comfort and please.

He opened her wider, bending her knees to make room for his broad shoulders. Then he kissed his way down her thighs, skipping over her sex so he could tease both sides before focusing on his target.

She pushed both hands into his hair, not tugging or guiding, just sifting the strands through her fingers. This was her night, so he allowed her to touch him any way she wanted.

Finally settling his lips over her slit, he inhaled her tantalizing scent, letting it soothe and arouse him. If her wetness was any indication of her need, she wouldn't last long once he touched her clit. So he teased her folds, circling her passage and sucking gently on the delicate flesh. She rocked her hips, pushing up with her heels to increase the pressure of his mouth.

He ignored her obvious need, parting her with his thumbs instead so he could fill her with his tongue. He needed to form the link. That was the reason for his actions. Well, one of the reasons. He also loved the taste of her arousal and the noises she made while he devoured her soft sex.

He closed his eyes and used the motion of his mouth to guide him into her mind. He penetrated carefully, slowly, pushing deeper both physically and metaphysically. She moaned, shuddering violently as his energy branched out, saturating her being with his intensity.

As he prepared to anchor the link, he felt compelled to ask her permission one last time. He was already in her mind, so audible words were no longer necessary. *Do you accept my claim? Will you be my anchor and my mate?*

Lily's eyes flew open as his questions echoed through her mind. She'd heard his voice inside her head before, but it was so much clearer now. Wanting to make sure he heard her, she spoke and thought her response. "Yes. I accept your claim. I want you as my mate and will gladly be your anchor."

He shifted his mouth slightly, catching her clit between his lips. Knowing what he was about to do, she closed her eyes and tried not to tense. He sucked gently at first, then with more urgency as distraction kept her orgasm at bay.

His lips released and his tongue took over, circling her clit just the way she liked. Still her stubborn climax remained just out of reach.

"Anchor the link. If I feel your emotions, it will make me come," she whispered.

Something shifted inside her mind and sensations blasted through her. Consuming desire and aching need exploded in a staggering burst. The intensity burned away her inhibitions and triggered her orgasm, just as she'd predicted. She came in hard, clenching waves, back bowed clear off the bed.

He lunged upward, joining their bodies with one sharp thrust. A pain sharp, yet fleeting, flashed through her mind and then there was only pleasure. She cried out and circled his waist with her legs. He started moving immediately, unable to hold himself back any longer.

She dragged his mouth down to hers, needing the tender intimacy of their kisses. His lips slanted over hers and he pushed into her mouth, her taste still strong on his tongue. Their emotions flowed from one mind to the other and back, weaving together so completely that one became indistinguishable from the other.

She unhooked her ankles and drew her legs up along his sides as his strokes lengthened and sped. She concentrated on where their bodies joined, savoring the erotic slide of his shaft as their emotions tumbled and swirled.

But now she could feel what Arton felt too, the firm grip of her inner muscles and the way her core seemed to hug him as he withdrew. It created an entirely new dimension to the exchange, making it more dynamic, more profound.

His kiss grew almost desperate and sexual hunger consumed rational thought. They strained and struggled, both determined to share themselves without reserve. They reached the end together, tumbling into sweet oblivion at the same time.

He cried out, clutching her to his chest as he buried his entire length inside her. She wrapped her arms and legs around him, clinging tightly as wave after powerful wave crashed down upon them. Pleasure pulsed on and on, stronger and more intense than anything either of them had ever experienced before.

Having only the strength to roll them to their sides, Arton collapsed, stunned yet replete. "I love you, mate," he whispered against her hair and tenderness flowed into her mind.

"I love you too, mate." It took her a moment to figure out how he'd done it, but she soon blanketed him with affection.

Say it again, but like this. I love you with all my heart and will love you as long as I live.

She closed her eyes and found their link, sending her thoughts for the very first time. *I love you more and I loved you first.*

Well, I love you better, he countered playfully.

She laughed, joy making her feel almost giddy. *I never dreamed this would happen to me. I thought it was impossible.*

Things only become impossible when people stop trying.

That wasn't always true, but it was a sweet sentiment and she was way too content right now to debate with him.

"Was Kage angry when you told him you were going to switch anchors? He had access to harbinger energy for a really long time." He tensed and dread trickled into her mind. She pushed back enough so she could see his face. "Why the dread? What happened?"

"I was still being stubborn, trying to protect you from my pain."

That surprised her. She thought Kage had been the one to take it badly. "What did you do, or what did he do?"

"I've never heard of anyone strong enough to do it, but he basically forced me out of his mind and destroyed the anchor bond." He shuddered and flashes of pain so intense it made her stomach heave radiated across their link. "It wasn't pleasant."

"That's what Skyla sensed when she healed you."

He nodded. "I'm anchored to my mate now. This is how it was meant to be, but damn that hurt."

She snuggled back into his warmth and returned her head to his shoulder. "Serves you right for being so stubborn. I'll have to thank the overlord next time I see him."

"Keep talking about Kage and I'll have to remind you that you belong to me and only me."

She grinned against his chest and said, "He is rather handsome."

With a predictable growl, he swept her beneath him and staked his claim on her eager body all over again.

ARTON WOKE UP SLOWLY late that evening. Lily was still curled against him, soundly asleep. But then it had been well into the afternoon before they satisfied their hunger for each other enough to rest. He carefully disentangled himself from her delightfully clingy arms and eased himself off the bed. He wanted to check in with Kage, let him know his rash impulse had worked and he'd be seeing very little of him or Lily for the next few days.

Half an hour later, Arton found the overlord on the observation platform enjoying a colorful sunset with Skyla. They exchanged conspirators' smiles as Arton approached. "You two look entirely too pleased with yourselves," he grumbled.

"Well, you look better than you did last night," Skyla said brightly.

"Did you sleep well?" Kage smirked and Arton wanted to slug him.

"You both know damn well that I claimed Lily. Just say congratulations."

"Congrats, brother." Kage surprised him further by giving him a bear hug that nearly crushed his ribs.

Skyla hugged him next and kissed him on the cheek. "May you make each other deliriously happy."

"Where's my father?" He didn't realize what he'd done until he saw Skyla's startled expression. He never referred to Kryton as father, at least not to his face. "Has he disowned me or something?"

She smiled, clearly thrilled by the change. "I just wish he'd been here to hear it."

"I suspect I'll slip again, so don't be too disappointed." Then he surprised her by returning the kiss on her cheek.

"If this is getting all sentimental, I'm leaving."

Arton laughed and waved him back. "I just came to give you the news and to explain why we'd both be MIA for the next few days."

"You have three days," Kage told him, "then I need Lily back in main medical assisting Dr. Foran. We only have Skyla for another two weeks. We must make the most of them."

"Understood." He looked at Skyla and smiled. "Tell my father I said hello."

"I will. And by the way, I already talked Kryton into a compromise and Kage here has approved it."

He looked at the overlord curiously. "What compromise?"

"The elder General Lux has agreed to keep our location secret from the younger General Lux if I allow Kryton to transport any female who wishes to leave back to Earth."

The deal was so shocking, Arton could only stare. What if half—or most—of the females decided to leave? The Outcast dream of a world all their own would crumble before it had time to take shape.

A world *all their own*? He was pretty damn sure this planet didn't qualify with or without the females.

"Spare me your wide-eyed shock," Kage said. "We both know we can't keep them if they really want to go home. I was just hoping to give their mates enough time to convince them that they wanted to stay."

"Then I propose another stipulation," Arton said, not yet ready to give up on the dream. Thanks to Lily, he was finally feeling part of things rather than an outsider looking in. The new perspective filled him with determination. This was a dream worthy of the fight. "Each female will be given the opportunity to leave, but only after she's met at least three of her potential matches. She needs to know what she's rejecting before she can make the best decision."

Skyla thought for a moment, lips pursed, gaze averted. Finally, she nodded and looked at Arton. "It will take some work, but I think I can get *your father* to agree."

"Good, now I'm going back to bed where my newly bonded mate is waiting for me." Just saying the phrase brought a happy smile to his lips.

"Have fun," Kage called.

Arton only waved, his thoughts already focused on the woman he loved and the future they would build together.

Epilogue

"**I**s turning you in to the elders the only way to curtail your reckless behavior?"

Isolaund Farr gasped and spun around at her brother's angry voice. Her battle cats growled, baring their teeth. She quickly sent a telepathic signal preventing them from attacking him. "Don't sneak up on me like that. I might not be able to stop them from ripping you to shreds next time." She tossed back the deep hood on her dark green cloak and pulled off her gloves.

"You've been to the surface again."

She didn't deny it. What was the point, this passage only led one place and that was topside. "The intruders ignored my warning. It's obvious they have no intention of leaving. We'll have to drive them off."

He made an impatient sound and fell into step beside her as she headed back toward her chambers. "It's forbidden to go above. You could end up in a stone cell if you don't stop obsessing over those fools. The guiding council knows about them and is deliberating on a plan."

"All they ever do is *deliberate*." She spat out the word with a snarl and tossed back her long silver hair. "I prefer action, decisive action."

"You really want to start a war?" he sounded incredulous. "Why not just share the planet with them. We've done so before."

"And that worked out so well for our grandparents," she snapped. "They were hunted to the verge of extinction and barely escaped Earth with their lives." She faced him, fists planted on her hips. "The females are human! Do you still want to share our world with them?"

He tensed, his arguments dissolving beneath the power of her righteous indignation. "You can't take them on all by yourself."

She laughed harshly and lengthened her strides. "Watch me!"

THE END—FOR NOW

If you enjoyed this book, please let me know by leaving a review.

Thanks so much, Cyndi

Up next in the Outcast saga:

Featuring Rex Dravon and Thea Cline

25825904R00136

Printed in Poland
by Amazon Fulfillment
Poland Sp. z o.o., Wrocław